BUT I WOULDN'T WANT TO *DIE* THERE

BUT I WOULDN'T WANT TO *DIE* THERE

A JENNY CAIN MYSTERY

Nancy Pickard

POCKET BOOKS

New York   London   Toronto   Sydney   Tokyo   Singapore

POCKET BOOKS, a division of Simon & Schuster Inc.
1230 Avenue of the Americas, New York, NY 10020

ISBN 0-671-72330-8

For my son, Nick

Thanks to Marilyn Wallace, Gillian Roberts, and Sarah Shankman for the title . . . to Jane Chelius for Brooklyn . . . to Dana Isaacson for roofs, rockets, and Robert's . . . to Susan Sandler for the Village . . . to Marilyn, Susan Dunlap, and Sally Goldenbaum for reading and critiquing . . . to thousands of New Yorkers for being your funny, cranky, brilliant, wired, angry, patient, hopeful, cynical, charming, annoying, endearing selves . . . to my agent, Meredith Bernstein, and my editor, Linda Marrow, for being my most excellent partners in business and friendship . . . and especially to Kay Marquet, the Jenny Cain of Sonoma County, Ca.

BUT I WOULDN'T WANT TO *DIE* THERE

Prologue

I CAN'T REMEMBER THE EXACT WORDS, BUT THE MESSAGE ON my telephone answering machine went something like this:

"Hi, pal." It was the familiar voice of my long-distance friend Carol Margolis. *"How's tricks in the sticks? Got to be better than it is here in the big city."* New York, she meant. *"Listen, I've got a problem for you to solve, Jenny. What if somebody you knew was doing something illegal? And what if this illegal thing they were doing could hurt other people and maybe already had harmed them in some way? But what if you believed in your heart that this was basically a good person who meant well, and what if this illegal act of theirs was also doing good for people? What would you do, hmm? Turn 'em in? Report them? And to further complicate the situation, what if by snitching on them, you'd ruin their life and really make a mess of your own, and you'd feel terrible about it and they'd hate you, and the people they were helping would hate you, and you'd feel incredibly guilty about the whole thing, even if none of it was your fault and they really were doing something wrong?"*

At that point, there was the sound of a sigh on the machine.

1

"Thanks, pal. Just telling you about it makes me realize what I have to do. I'll talk to you some other time, Jenny. You don't have to call me back."

Of course, I was going to call her back anyway.

But I was busy that week, so I didn't.

1

ONE WEEK LATER, IT WAS HER BOSS WHO BROKE THE NEWS to me that my friend Carol Margolis was dead. This message I took in person, when Carol's boss called from a law office in New York City to my home in Port Frederick, Massachusetts.

"Jenny Cain?" she asked.

"Yes," I confirmed.

"This is Patricia Vinitsky," she announced. I heard New York City in the accent and a faraway familiarity in the name. "I'm president of the board of the Hart Foundation. I believe you . . . uh, have been a friend of our . . . uh, director, Carol Margolis."

"Why, yes," I said enthusiastically and unsuspectingly.

"I gather you don't know, and I regret to tell you, that Carol is dead; she was killed in a street robbery one night last week. I'm sorry nobody thought to inform you before this. Her parents probably didn't know how to reach you, and her husband . . . well, you know how Steve is . . ."

"No, I—"

Didn't want to know. Any part of this. Wanted it to stop. Wanted to go back to when my phone rang, and wanted to refuse to answer it.

"Carol . . ." I said.

3

We'd become friends because we held twin jobs as directors of community foundations. We'd met at a convention, and we'd hit it off immediately. Then we'd commenced that sort of rare, intense friendship that you can usually only conduct with somebody you see infrequently. At those times—usually at conventions—we'd share a year's worth of gossip and intimacy and hilarity. If we'd been lovers, we'd have wanted to see each other more often; since we were friends, it was enough to share a room once a year and to talk by phone. Although we were separated by time and space, Carol Margolis was one of my best friends. Even so, I hadn't spoken to her since right after my mother died; she'd left that last message and a couple of earlier innocuous ones that I hadn't gotten around to returning; I'd been preoccupied, I'd known that she would understand, I hadn't known it would matter. I had thought I'd be seeing her at the next convention or talking to her soon on the phone . . .

Vinitsky's next words slipped past me like cars sliding downhill in an earthquake. I grasped the horror of it and wanted to reach out and stop them, but I was helpless to do anything more than observe it all in a silence of shock.

"It happened on West End Avenue. She was running like she did every evening. Some bastard tried to rob her, that's what they're saying, but she wasn't carrying anything, no money, not even wearing a watch, not even a fanny pack. She'd taken along enough money for coffee at a place she liked, but she'd already spent that, she'd already had the coffee. The son of a bitch got her three blocks from there, when she was almost home. He stabbed her, left her to bleed to death on the sidewalk. She was screaming after he ran away, listen I'm sorry to tell you all this, maybe you don't want to know the details, but I thought you'd want to hear that people did try to help, they did come, even the paramedics, but nobody could help her."

I was silent, stunned. Nothing to say. No questions. I was thinking of her last message to me. I wanted desperately now to call her back, *Please, let me call you back, Carol* . . .

"You're a foundation director, too?"

"What?" The tears were starting to flow, and I thought: *What is this chitchat? Give it a pass. Let me off the phone, so I can cry my cry, feel my sorrow for my murdered friend.* "What? Wait." I grabbed a tissue from the pocket of the sweatshirt I was wearing over blue jeans, and I held the phone away from my face while I blew my nose and wiped my cheeks. Impatiently, I said, "I was, yes."

"We need somebody to fill in," Vinitsky said. "We're in a hell of a bind since Carol died. Things are happening. One crisis after another, you know?"

"Yeah," I said, and I did know. That's the norm in foundation work: one emergency following another as naturally as blood flows from an open wound. My desire to hang up the phone was more urgent than any crisis she had, and so I was slow to grasp her meaning. And then I did, unbelieving. "You're kidding."

"We need an interim director until we hire somebody permanently. Maybe you'd like to take over till then? For a salary and all expenses. Make it a tryout for the job, if you like. That'd certainly be fine with us. You can even stay in Carol's place. I don't know if you knew that she and Steve were separated, but he says he doesn't want to live there now, and he says you're welcome to use it while you're in town—"

"Wait!" I blew my nose again, closer to the phone this time. How dare she? *Hey, listen, your buddy's dead, you want her job?* I swallowed phlegm and tears and anger before I spoke again. "Stop. This is too quick. Too much." So why, if I were really so offended, did I add the next sentence, the one that opened the door to a most dangerous decision? "And even if it weren't, you don't know anything about me."

"Yes, I do," Vinitsky said, and now the door was fully open, and fate began to come rushing in at me. "I know that you very recently quit the Port Frederick Civic Foundation, where you worked for a long time, and I know that you're presently unemployed. I know that Carol spoke highly of you and I know that we modeled some of our programs on ones you started up there in wherever the hell you are in Massachusetts. And I know that when I called around the country, your name was the one that came up most frequently in conversations with other people in foundation work. They said you'd be great for the job." She added quickly, "For this interim position. Will you come? For Carol? Like tomorrow?"

"For *Carol?*"

"Frankly, she left us some problems."

Ah, better than flowers, I thought, better than a contribution to a favorite charity. "The family requests that friends step in to clean up the messes left by the dearly beloved deceased." This was crazy. But it would be a temporary job until I figured out what I wanted to be when I grew up. In the city I loved the most in the world, doing the kind of work that had me hooked. As a tribute, a memorial, in a weird way, to a dear friend, a dead friend . . .

"I can't believe I'm saying this, but go ahead and tell me more, especially the part about those crises you mentioned, those 'things that are happening' . . ."

Long distance, Pat Vinitsky, attorney, president of the board of the Hart Foundation, and my future "interim" boss, sighed. "Okay, how about the rich old lady who has changed her mind about leaving her fortune to the foundation? That's one. And how about the man who's so mad at us that he wants to sue us to get back the money he already gave us? That's two. Then there's the amateur theater down in the Village that didn't get the last installment of their grant money because Carol didn't get the check to them on time. Don't ask me why, that's for you to find out. And there's a little literacy project, a fabulous project, that I want funded as soon as possible, but I need somebody to run another site evaluation. That's the sort of stuff I mean, like that."

I had nearly smiled through my tears during her recital.

It all sounded so familiar, so enticingly challenging and infuriating and satisfying. Almost cozy. I could do this. With my eyes closed and my hands tied behind my back with red tape. I could do it for Carol. Hell, who was I kidding? I'd be doing it for myself as well.

"I'll get back to you," I told Vinitsky.

That got her off the phone.

So that finally I could sit down and cry . . . and remember that last message of Carol's. *What had she said? Problems? Somebody doing something illegal? And they'd hate her if she turned them in? And that it might ruin their life and mess up hers, too?* Was that what she'd said? Another emotion flooded in upon my sorrow, and from the hair that raised on my scalp and arms, I recognized it as horror.

"Did this problem only mess up your life, Carol?" I asked

my murdered friend, through my tears for her. "Or did it end it?"

"About all you can do," suggested my husband the cop, "is to call New York, find out a name of a homicide detective assigned to Carol's case, and tell him—or her—about the message."

"There is one other thing I can do," I said.

Geof, who is a lieutenant with the Port Frederick police force, cocked his head, waiting for what I was going to say next.

"I can take this interim job."

"I hate New York," he said.

"Is that pertinent?"

"If you decide to take that job, you lose me."

I stared at him. "Did I miss something here? Or have we just jumped from point A to point Z without any logical progression in between? Nobody said anything about making this permanent." At the look on his face, I conceded, "All right, maybe Vinitsky did mention that as a possibility, but that doesn't mean I'd want to do it. Geof, I didn't know you felt that strongly about my taking a job out of town, especially in that town."

"Well, now you know."

"No compromises?" I was horrified at the turn this simple conversation had taken. "If I do this, I'll only be gone a little while, and I won't make any decisions without you, surely you know that."

He didn't seem to think there was anything to discuss.

"I will not live in New York," he stated. "I will not commute to New York to live with you part-time. I will not be a good sport if you want to be the one to do the commuting. I want you, not a frequent flyer coupon. That's it, Jenny, that's how I feel."

"You're not being fair, Geof."

"And you think you are?"

"How can you say that? I haven't taken the job!"

"You will. I know you. You love New York."

"Oh, you *know*, do you?" I took a deep breath, trying to calm down. He was panicking, that was it, at the idea that our

7

lives might change, and dramatically, before he was ready for it. Everything had been in a state of flux in the months since my mother died, since I'd quit my longtime job, since he'd been suspended from the force for the time he'd spent in helping me to investigate my mother's life and death. He was back at work now, and I was looking for work. We'd been firmly together during all those difficult times; it was only now, during the transition between then and . . . the future . . . that tension was building between us again, so that a marriage that once felt so firm now seemed at risk of falling apart. We went through periods of rockiness, didn't every marriage? The scary part was that you never knew when one of those periods might end up throwing your partnership *on* the rocks, splintered, shattered, irretrievable. Surely, this wasn't it! Not after everything else we'd been through. It was worth pleading for, no matter who was right or wrong. "Listen, I really do want to take this interim job, I'm sorry, but I do, for Carol's sake if nothing else. It'll only be for a few weeks, maybe only two or three. You could come spend the weekends with me. It'll be like a little vacation. Please? Even if you think you'll hate it? We'll have a good time. We'll talk about it then."

"I won't change my mind."

"Oh, well, good!" I was suddenly furious at him. "Just so we know where we stand!" I held up my hands appeasingly. "Sorry, sorry! Okay, but you'll come?"

His answer was unexpected, welcome, infuriating.

"I love you," my husband confessed, "it's New York I hate."

"You'll do it?"

"I'll do it."

"We appreciate your calling," the New York homicide detective said to me, "especially long distance like this. I understand she was a good friend of yours, and you want to help. But you got to understand, this looks like a classic street mugging. She was running, he stopped her, he asked her for money, she told him she didn't have any, and so he stuck her for no good reason."

"But maybe there was a reason—"

8

BUT I WOULDN'T WANT TO *DIE* THERE

"No," he said patiently, "you don't understand, there's never a good reason for a crime like this. There doesn't have to be. It just happens, and this time it happened to your friend. Listen, I'm sorry."

"But you'll—"

"Of course, we'll see what we can do with this information, but don't get your hopes up."

I thought that was a silly thing to say. It was too late for hope, that wasn't what I was after; I was after revenge and resolution, and I was going to New York City to search for it.

2

THE FIRST TIME I EVER VISITED NEW YORK CITY BY MYSELF
I figured that if I could just make it alive from the airport into
Manhattan, I'd survive the rest of the trip.

You know how that feels, that outsider's fear of New York?

It's the feeling of being so naive when you step off the air-
plane, as if everybody around you is a native and you're the
only tourist. And it's all those tales you've heard about stolen
luggage and crazy cab drivers and women who steal purses off
hooks on the backs of toilet stalls. And it's that intimidating
business of mastering the queue for the cabs outside the airport
and of debating whether you're supposed to tip the person who
growls, "Where to?" and whistles a taxi down the line to you.
And it's how dumb you feel the first time, when everybody
else in the cab line is talking in code, saying things like "midtown," "SoHo," or "the Village." And it's watching strangers
match up for shared rides and wondering if you're supposed to
do that, too, and how do they manage the fare and will you get
stuck for paying for a whole ride when you only ought to pay
for a quarter of the bill?

And it's the rotting shells of cars along the expressways, the
unintelligible graffitti on the underbellies of the underpasses,
and the surprise when the cab driver asks you if you want to

10

pay the bridge toll now or later, and you think in a panic, *What bridge toll!?* and you don't want him to know that you don't know which is the smarter choice, because you don't want *anybody* to know you're from out of town. And so you say, "Later," and you could swear that he smirks into his rearview mirror, and you figure that means that he knows he's got a live one and that you've just agreed to pay the equivalent of taxi fare to Nova Scotia on a Saturday night.

But then it happens, just about the time you get past Hell's Gate and the cabbie drives you onto the Triborough Bridge, just about then, when all seems lost and you figure you'll never see your loved ones again in this lifetime, you get your first glimpse of the skyline of Manhattan. *Oh! There's the Empire State Building! And isn't that the World Trade Center?* And then you're rocketing south down East River Drive, and he whips a right onto Seventy-second Street, and suddenly you're crossing First Avenue, Second Avenue, Third, Lexington, Park, Madison, Fifth. *And there's Central Park! And, oh my God, he's going to drive straight through the park, we'll be killed!*

But no, dozens of cars are driving through the beautiful green park alongside of you and in front of you and behind you, and some of those people are smiling and talking, and they look as if they know what they're doing, so you relax a little.

And then there's your hotel or your friend's building or the restaurant where you're supposed to meet somebody, and you manage to compute the tip and you remember to get a receipt and the driver smiles at you and says what you figure is probably the Islamic equivalent of "have a nice day," and all of a sudden you're having just that, better than that, all of that, and more.

New York City!

You've done it, you've mastered the trip into town, and now everything's going to be fine. You'll live and maybe not even to regret it. You're thrilled! You're here. *Here.* You're empress of the universe and at least as sophisticated as the average ten-year-old from the Bronx.

This wasn't my virgin trip to New York City.
But I was nearly as nervous as the first time.

11

"Upper West Side," I told the taxi driver when I slid into his back seat outside LaGuardia Airport. I could speak the lingo now, even adding, "Eightieth and Riverside Drive," in proper cross-street speak.

The driver said, "My darling, if I could, I would take you in my arms and fly you there." *Welcome to New York,* I thought, *where everybody's a stranger, and nobody is.* Frankly, the way he drove, flying would have been my preference, too.

I was nervous enough already.

By the time he swooped in for a "landing" in front of my destination, I was sweating inside my black trench coat, my black wool business suit and black silk blouse, and my red silk underwear. Even the soles of my feet were sweating inside my black hose and my black business pumps. Black was hip in Manhattan this year, or so I'd been told by a New York friend who had also admitted to me, "I went to dinner with my husband the other night. We were both wearing black. When we looked around in the restaurant, we saw that every single person there was also wearing black!" Me, too. Like most tourists, I wanted to pass for a native.

Outside the cab, standing on the curb with my suitcases, I craned my neck and gazed unabashedly, unashamedly, gawkingly, up at the elegant nineteenth-century brownstone building in front of me. It would be my home for a week, maybe two, or maybe even longer than that. The sight of it made my pulse race and tears gather in my eyes for reasons having nothing to do with the architecture. *Could I do this? Could I really move into the apartment of a murdered friend? Was I really stepping into her home, taking over her job? Granted, it was only tempo-rary*—maybe *only temporary*—but still . . .

"Carol," I said, under my breath. "I miss you."

Was I being a good friend or a ghoul?

It was early May, around ten in the morning, and (despite my fear-sweat) cooler in New York than it had been back home. The sunshine stole quick glances at me between the buildings as gray clouds raced along as if they were in a hurry to catch a commuter train. Light traffic rattled at my back, subways rumbled at my feet, boats moaned to each other on the rivers. New York City was the world's biggest vibrator: Everything

vibrated above, and below the streets. I got the feeling that all
those vibrations were the sound of millions of emotions mani-
festing themselves right smack dab into physical reality. Emotion: vibration: POP: reality. New York was an idea, I thought,
an idea held simultaneously by thirteen million people. What
if we all closed our eyes and thought about something else for
a moment: Would the city disappear?

It was clearly visible at this second.

Riverside Drive, where I stood with my luggage and my
misgivings, was a quiet two-lane street at this point, with Riverside Park just on the other side of it and a highway and the
Hudson River beyond that. I stared across at the park and saw
a caged dog run, a caged basketball court, a caged handball
court, a caged tennis court, a caged playground, a caged sand-
box. All around me on this side of the street were tall buildings
with small rooms within them. Cages within cages within cages.
Outside the basketball court, a black man with spindly legs in
blue trousers rifled through an overflowing trash basket. He
wasn't in a cage, so who was free?

Carol was, my friend Carol Margolis.

Now she had the freedom of the dead.

*Or was she caged, too, by a desire for revenge or by a long-
ing for her life or by the same urgent need I felt to know who
killed her and why they'd chosen to stab her, beautiful, brilliant
her, on a New York evening? Carol probably knew the answer
to that one. Surely the dead know who kills them, maybe they
even understand the why that leads to forgiving.*

Not me.

"Hello, New York," I said out loud.

I took a deep, fetid breath of her, of the fragrance of the
fresh flowers in her stalls along the avenues and of the stench
of her warm urine wafting up from the subway through the
grates in her sidewalks and the aroma of her Italian bread rising
to crusty perfection in her bakeries and the stink of her dog
shit in the laughable little squares of dirt that surrounded her
pathetic trees and the sharp tang of her chic women and the
musk of her rich men and the fumes of her limos idling at her
curbs and the wet rotting odor of her cardboard shacks. I took
it all in, and I announced for her to hear, because I knew

she was accustomed to eavesdropping as her citizens talked to themselves and to her: "I'm Jenny Cain, and for the next couple of weeks, you are *mine*."

"Sounds good to me," said a young doorman. He hoisted all my luggage and grinned down at me from a great gawky, pimpled teenaged height. "So, like, when do we start?"

3

T HE YOUNG DOORMAN—HIS NAMETAG SAID JED—LED ME
down three cement steps to a small, dark, boxlike entry that
opened onto a long, shadowy hallway. The front door was ajar,
so he pushed it open, doing the same with the next door, and
managing to hold it all for me and my luggage. I sidled on in
ahead of him and stared around me.

"Who you stayin' with?" he inquired.

I glanced back at him and smiled but didn't answer.

Carol's name was stuck in my throat.

Jed was eccentrically attired, as if he'd dressed himself from
a Salvation Army clothes rack: a gray tailcoat too long at the
wrists, with tails that flopped at the backs of his knees; a Pearl
Jam T-shirt; blue jeans tucked into black leather riding boots.
He was around eighteen years old, I guessed, and craggy and
pimply faced, with long curly brown hair just barely tamped
down by a gray chauffeur's cap.

"All this stuff," he said, "looks like you're stayin' awhile."

He set down my luggage with an audible groan.

"God, you pack your weights in here? No, but hey, that's
good. Maybe you'll like it here, so you'll want to buy into the
building. We could use a couple new owners, get rid of a couple
more old ones."

"I'm staying in Carol Margolis's place."

Jed stared, mouth open. "No shit?"

I indicated that was the case.

"God," he said, all teenage boy now, "that was awful, wasn't it? Her gettin' killed and shit? She a friend of yours?"

I indicated that, too, was the case.

"God, it was tragic! Just a couple blocks from here, did you know that?"

I shook my head: *No*.

"Yeah, I mean, what's the world coming to? There are some not nice people in it these days, you know? I wasn't on duty, but one of the tenants, he said he heard the screaming clear over here. Awful, awful, I can't hardly stand to think about it." Jed's arms and legs were dancing now, twitching, nervously moving all the time he spoke, as if the story made him feel too uptight to hold still. In his gray tails, he looked like an aberrant, ungainly Fred Astaire. "Was it her screaming? That's what I asked him, but he says, how's he supposed to know what some-body sounds like when they're screaming? He's never heard any of the tenants scream before, he says, to which I says, Hey, you livin' in a different building from me, you never hear any tenants screaming? I hear them yelling at each other all the time and it ain't any two blocks away either." He slapped his own face with both hands, as if to get his own attention. "So what are you doin', you gonna rent her place?"

"I'm taking her job temporarily until they fill it."

"No shit?" Jed sniffed, raising his right nostril to do it and then twinned the act with his left. It seemed to help him think, to calm down his compulsive movements. "So what do you think? You like the looks of this little joint?"

"It's beautiful," I said, fully meaning it.

The hallway that served as a lobby looked more like the foyer of an elegant private home than the commercial property it really was. The walls were painted an immaculate white with bright yellow woodwork trim; a polished wooden banister trailed alongside a long marble stairway to a second floor. The bright light paint helped the atmosphere, because, basically, it was a shadowy house, narrow, with stairways casting shadows on floors and walls throwing shadows across halls. When I peered up, I saw the landings of several more floors above us.

16

Flower prints, framed and glassed, adorned the walls abutting the stairway. There was a single door to my right, as we entered, and a second door way on down the front hall, almost under the stairs.

"Little piece of paradise," Jed agreed. "Mom keeps it nice."

I turned to look up at him. "Your mother."

"Owns the joint," he said, casually. "Old family mansion. Rents some rooms on a yearly basis, rents the others out as bed and breakfast. Kinda unusual, I guess, but then so is my mom. That's how Carol Margolis and Steve Wolff found this place, you know?"

Again, I shook my head: *No.*

"Yeah, they stayed here on their honeymoon and just kinda never left. The bad news is, we gotta climb. You're on the fifth. No elevators. Heave ho.

I took one of my three bags away from Jed, so that he wouldn't have to carry all of them, and together we trudged upward.

"When's the last time you saw her, Jed?"

"Earlier that day."

"Did she seem okay to you?"

He glanced back at me. "Okay? Like, what'd you mean?"

"I mean, was she smiling, happy?"

"Oh, I see what you mean, yeah, it'd be nice to think that, that she had a nice day, her last day. I guess so, sure, if it makes you happy."

It was hardly a satisfying answer, as it didn't suggest whether Carol might have looked worried or frightened about anything that afternoon before her death.

We were moving past a floor with three doors.

One of them was open, with classical music streaming out, and I thought I recognized the piercing sweet violin of Dvorak chamber music. I paused to catch my breath, to steal a listen.

I glanced within that apartment and gasped in panic.

"*Jed!*" It came out a whispered scream.

He looked, saw what I saw, put down my bags, and said to me perfectly calmly and without missing a beat, "I can handle this. Don't move." If his voice expressed any emotion at all, it was only annoyance.

My emotions were running riot, however.

What I saw was a naked, pudgy elderly woman straddling the sill of an open window. One bare dimpled leg hung down inside her living room, the other was out of my sight on the other side of the window. The achingly lovely music was sliding into the air from a cassette player plugged into an outlet on the floor near her. The small bare foot was beating a rhythm in time to the piano.

Jed strolled into the room as if he had all the time in the world.

Hurry! I yelled at him in my head.

I was a nervous wreck by the time he reached her side. Jed stuck his hands in his pants pockets and said in a conversational tone, "Mrs. Amory, you got to turn the music down, it's bothering the other owners." She was mesmerized by something outside or possibly something internal and didn't even look up. Jed turned then, noticed a bathrobe on the back of a chair, picked it up, and walked it back over to her, draping it over her naked body right there in the window. "Better come in now, Mrs. Amory," he said in that same easy conversational tone, "before you get arrested. Grab my arm, that's it. Okay, now the robe. You really embarrass me when you do this, you know that? You might think how you make me feel now and then. I'm only nineteen years old, for Chrissake. Is this anything for a young man such as myself to have to deal with? You might think about that while you're lookin' out the fuckin' window. Excuse me, but really, it just bothers me a lot, and I think you ought to know that. And it pisses my mother off, and you don't want to do that, do you? Oh, hell, you're not listening, do you ever listen, Mrs. Amory? You're not ever really going to jump, are you? You wouldn't do that to me, would you?"

Jed sat her down in a chair, then closed her window with a decisive thump and locked it, applying so much force that I wondered if the old woman could get it open again. He left her draperies wide, but he turned to her, as he bent down to lower the volume on the radio, and he said warningly, "Stay dressed, okay? Window down. Clothes on. That's our deal. You want to get naked, that's fine, but first you close your drapes and shut your door. Okay, Mrs. Amory, I'm going to be walking up and down this hall all day, and I'm going to be lookin' up at your window from outside, too, and I don't want to have this problem with you again. Got that?"

She stiffened her chin like a stubborn child and glared at me.

Jed left her there and rejoined me, closing her door on his way out.

"Man, I'm tired of this shit," he said, but he didn't look at me, just grabbed my two bags again, and started on up to the third floor.

"What was that all about?" I asked, behind him.

"It's about me gettin' out of this nuthouse," he snapped.

"It really frightened me when I saw her."

"Sorry."

"No, I don't mean that, it's not your fault . . . I was just saying, it scared me. My heart's still pounding." I lowered my voice. It wasn't easy to talk and breathe at the same time, carrying a bag on the steep stairway. "Is she crazy, Jed? Or senile? Shouldn't she be in a hospital?"

"I got nothin' to say about it."

There were three closed doors on the third floor and two closed doors on the fourth. Breathing hard and moving much more slowly, we reached the fifth, where Jed dumped my bags in front of a door labeled 5A below its peephole. On my floor, there was also a 5B and a 5C.

I looked up at him, but he was avoiding my gaze now.

"You were good with her," I said.

"I got lots of practice," he muttered as he placed a key in a lock.

"Are you going to notify somebody?"

"Yeah. My mother."

When he didn't volunteer any other information, I looked around the fifth floor. "Do I have neighbors behind those other doors?"

He smiled a little as he turned the key and then inserted a second key into a second lock. "Oh, yes, you got neighbors, you most certainly do have neighbors." He opened the door a crack and then handed me a separate ring containing three keys. I thought of how people hardly bothered to lock their doors in Port Frederick, and here Jed and I had passed through two multiply-locked doors downstairs and two locks on this inner door. "Here," he instructed, "these are yours. Big one's

19

for the doors downstairs, middle one's for this top lock, little one's for this bottom lock. You got a chain and a bolt on the inside of this door, too. When you got visitors, they can buzz you and you can go down and let them in, or they can buzz me, and I'll call you for permission to let them up. I'm the door just to the right as we came in downstairs. That's my place. Mom's on down the hall, but you won't need to bother her. I'm the one you want."

Just as he put out his hand to push my door open, the other two doors on the floor opened simultaneously. Out of 5C peered a wizened male face. Out of 5B emerged a woman's face, equally old but considerably sweeter in expression. That one was followed by a thin little body wrapped in slacks and a skirt and three cardigan sweaters, all buttoned from waist to neck, with their various clashing colors peeking through between the buttons. Her painfully thin blue-veined hands held a round brown cake, dribbled with white icing, on a plate, and her thin little face, topped by a red kerchief wrapped around her white hair, held a shy smile.

She held out the cake to me.

I took it, and she flashed a sweet smile and then slipped back into her apartment and quietly closed her door. I heard bolts turning.

"Hi, Mrs. Golding!" Jed called out loudly to her closed door. "This is Jenny Cain, the one who's going to live in Ms. Margolis's apartment for a while! She was a good friend of Ms. Margolis, so it's okay, her being here! Thanks for bakin' her the nice cake!"

He said to me, nodding at the closed door, "Mrs. Ida Golding."

Taking his cue, I spoke to the door, *"Thank you very much!"*

Jed nodded toward the baleful old face of the man who was still peering out of the door of 5C. "Hi, Mr. Bread. This is Ms. Cain." To me, he said, "That's Mr. Daley Bread."

As in old and crusty? I wondered.

The old man slammed his door.

"What is this place?" I whispered. "A nursing home?"

Jed pushed wide the door to Carol's apartment and laughed as he did so. "Nah. Ms. Margolis and Mr. Wolff weren't old and decrepit. And I'm not. And you're not. And my mom's not.

And a couple of other tenants aren't. So, no, it's not exactly what you'd call a nursing home. So, here's your place, how do you like it?"

At the sight of the rooms that he revealed to me, a choked "Oh!" escaped from my throat. It was an exclamation of sadness, an "oh" of pain and pleasure, all in one.

"Looks like her, doesn't it?" Jed said.

I could only nod in agreement and step inside where everything was peaches and cream, just like Carol, who'd been a very feminine woman. There was a large living room, which appeared to double as the only bedroom, with an apparent sofa bed upholstered in a fabric with peach dahlias and creamy poppies, a couple of yellow wicker rocking chairs with matching coffee and end tables and a white wicker magazine stand. I saw a round breakfast table with two chairs and a large chest of drawers topped by a scrolled mirror. The wood furniture looked like good but fairly inexpensive antiques, nineteenth century, maybe early twentieth. She'd had her walls painted a pale iris blue and the woodwork a satiny peach. It was all flowers and pillows, yellows and pinks, oranges and ivory. There were Oriental pewter bowls filled with potpourri and a soft, unobtrusive floral scent to the apartment. To the left I saw a tiny kitchen with appliances all in a row, and beyond the living/bedroom I could see a big white porcelain bathroom, with a large closet at the back. That seemed to be the extent of Carol's home; it was a lot smaller than I was accustomed to in the two-story "cottage" that Geof and I shared back home in Port Frederick.

Jed followed me, set down my bags, and moved quickly to the single long window in the living room. He pushed back the white eyelet draperies and proceeded to open the window as high as his shoulders. When I saw there was no screen on the window and that there was only thin air separating him from sudden death five stories below, a shallow wave of vertigo struck me, making the backs of my lower legs tingle and scooping out a hollow place in my abdomen. Instinctively, I put out my hands, as if to catch myself from falling.

"Put it back down a little, will you, Jed?"

"How much?" He lowered it until I said, "There."

He walked back toward me, and I fished out a five-dollar bill to hand him. "Scared you'll fall out?" he asked me, grinning now. "And I won't be here to save you? Hey, thanks."

"You're welcome, Jed. Thank *you*."

He didn't move for a moment, and then he said, speaking more to the floor at his feet than to me, "I wasn't there to save *her*." He looked up, his smile faded. "She was a nice lady. I hate it they killed her."

"Who, Jed?"

"Them!" He looked angry, discouraged, too old for his nineteen years. "They're everywhere, and there's nothing you can do to stop them. The bad guys. The assholes. They'll get us. They'll win in the end. You don't know, you're not from here, but they're all over this city. You'll find out. And they're going to win. In the end, they'll get us all, you, me, Mrs. Amory—they've almost got her now—everybody."

I felt relieved when he was gone.

What a morning! What a city! Where taxi drivers offered to fly me across town, pessimistic young kids saved naked old women from suicide, and shy strangers handed me home-baked cakes.

Who said New Yorkers didn't have a heart?

I leaned my back against the door to get a good look at the apartment that would be my living quarters for awhile . . . maybe longer. "My God, Carol," I said softly, "what a strange, fantastic experience this is going to be." *Going to be?* answered a voice in my head. *How about is already?*

"I need to sit down," I said, and so I did in her wicker rocking chair.

"You here?" I asked the air around me and then very softly, "Yo! Carol? This okay with you? Me being here? Taking your apartment? Taking your job?" Bitterly I added, "You being dead?"

A breeze ruffled the curtains at the long window.

I didn't know whether to take that as a ghostly yes or no, but I figured that a negative answer would come more violently—the window slamming down or the bathroom door crashing shut.

"So, okay," I said tentatively to both of us. "So, they say a stranger killed you on the street. So maybe that's what happened or maybe not. Let's find out." I glanced at the curtains.

"Better yet, why don't you just tell me and save us a lot of time? Swish the curtains one through twenty-six times for every letter of the alphabet. Or maybe a Ouija board?"

I was still holding my neighbor's cake, so I got up from the chair and walked over to the kitchen to deposit the cake on a counter. "We've got interesting neighbors, Carol," I said. "Mrs. Amory, Mrs. Golding, Daley Bread. And what's the matter with young Jed? Why is he so twitchy? Yeah, okay, maybe we would be, too, if we never knew when we would have to be yanking old ladies off window ledges. I get your point. Thank you."

Curious about everything, including my new domain, I started pulling open drawers and doors to check the supplies on hand: coffee, sugar, spices and seasonings, silverware, dishes, cups and glasses, pots and pans. All the basics, as if Carol and Steve were still living here.

"So what was the problem with Steve, Carol?" I asked the air.

It made me feel bad that she hadn't called me to talk about it. I guessed that she wanted to avoid dumping her problems on me because of what I was going through after my mother's death. Worse, that probably left her with nobody to talk to because she'd always said that Steve was her best friend and so, as a consequence, she didn't need buddies. There'd been me, sure, but even I was long-distance and low-maintenance.

Mrs. Golding's cake appeared to inch closer to me, inviting me to sample it. I withdrew a knife from a drawer and sliced a chunk off. It was delicious. I cut off another chunk and chewed that while I thought about how little I knew about Carol's widower, Steven Wolff. I'd met him only once, briefly, over dinner at some forgettable convention in some forgettable city. I remembered curly hair. Jewish, like Carol. Funny. Sarcastic. Very New York. Energy. A crackling quality. And the same sort of quality in the air between them. Were they having an argument that night, was that what I remembered?

"Can't remember." I shrugged and thought harder.

They fought a lot, I remembered Carol talking about that, but they loved a lot, too. Or used to. He was a musician, that much I knew, but he didn't make much money at it, I believed. She thought he was wonderfully talented, her parents didn't like him much, and what else? Why was she leaving the marriage? I thought back to my last conversation with her when she'd said (I thought), "He's driving me crazy, we fight all the time, we don't have any fun anymore, I'm getting out of this!" Or maybe that was what other friends of mine had said before *their* divorces?

Inside the refrigerator, I discovered a lovely surprise: a wicker basket loaded with goodies—bagels, muffins, tiny loaves of bread, an apple, an orange, a stick of butter, a cut-glass jar of purple jam, a dish of cream cheese, a tub of fruit yogurt. There was also a half-gallon of whole milk, a half-gallon of orange juice, and a half-pint of coffee cream. Who was responsible for this display of graciousness, I wondered? I suspected shy Mrs. Golding, of the chocolate cake, but then I hadn't met Jed's mother yet, and it could have been she.

"Thank you, whoever. So this is the big, bad city."

My husband would never believe it. As Geof had made all too clear before I left town, he thought New Yorkers knew only two words, and the second one was "you." I felt a twang of self-pity, which I traced to the fact that he didn't understand me and which called for the indulgence of another bite of cake.

As I ate it, I wandered through the spacious, high-ceilinged rooms. Besides the big bathroom, I found two huge walk-in closets, the largest of which had been converted into a tiny office complete with desk, computer, file cabinet, chair, bulletin board, and a telephone with an answering machine attached to it.

I punched the button labeled ANNC.

Carol's voice suddenly filled the little office.

"You've reached the Hart Foundation. Carol Margolis speaking. Sorry I can't take your call right now. If you'll leave a message at the beep, I'll get right back to you."

"Oh, no you won't," I said angrily.

I punched it five more times, probing my own wound, sticking a finger into the raw tissue to see how bad I could hurt myself, to test if I could make myself cry. It worked, all right. It took me several seconds to realize the doorbell was ringing, and I was still wiping my eyes when I opened the door to find her widower standing there.

4

I WAS TAKEN ABACK TO RECOGNIZE STEVE WOLFF ON THE threshold, and the startling suddenness of his appearance tempered the warmth of my greeting. Rather ungraciously, I welcomed him by blurting, "Steve? Isn't Jed supposed to tell me when I have a visitor?"

The stocky, curly-headed teddy bear standing in front of me, dressed in black denim pants and buttoned jacket, with his hands full of a large white envelope, replied in a tone that slid rapidly from friendly equanimity into a vehement whine. "Jed knows me. Which is more than my in-laws know. How is it that a man's doorman can know him better, more intimately, more accurately, than his own in-laws do?"

He barged past me into the living room where he and Carol had once lived together. Steve seemed to trail frizzly tendrils of energy in his wake. I remembered that about him, and I recognized it as that kind of uniquely New York energy that makes everybody else living anywhere else—even L.A.—feel slow and sluggish. When you find it—or feel it—it sticks out, looking a little dangerous, like a frayed electrical cord. He whirled to face me, like a cord whipping around, so that I involuntarily flinched.

"Does that seem right to you? Does that seem to be the

correct proportion to things? I don't think so. You ask me, it makes big things look small and small things look monstrous. It makes black white and white black and it turns gray to muddy brown. Don't mind me, I'm obsessed." He had started pacing the room while he ranted, looking things over, picking items up and setting them back down again, but precisely, with care, in their same places. "Maybe it's a stage of grief: shock, anger, sorrow, acceptance, obsession. I seem to have skipped acceptance. Acceptance sucks. Fuck acceptance. I'm supposed to accept it that Carol's dead? I'm supposed to fucking accept it that some asshole couldn't get it up except with a knife? Yeah, right! I'll accept his fucking head on a platter, that's what I'll accept. I'll accept him ripped to shreds by sharks. Fucking city." This was more like it, I thought while I watched him; Geof would believe this.

Steve very abruptly walked up to me and stared right at me. I held my ground. I saw tears spring to his brown eyes; he blinked them away and gave me a twisted smile.

"Hi, Jenny, it's nice to see you again. Kind of. You'll pardon my lack of wholehearted welcome. It ain't you, of course. It's the circumstances. Don't you love circumstances? And situations. So nicely polite and vague, like my in-laws. You'd think they were *goyem*, no offense to you nice gentile girls, I've always been partial to blonds, myself." He freed one of his hands by hiking the large white envelope up under his other armpit. With the freed hand, he reached out and tweaked a strand of my hair but then just as quickly let go of it, before I even had time to step back. "You ever meet my in-laws? Under the *cir*cumstances, Stevie, considering the situation, Stevé, go fuck yourself, Stevie." He cocked his head to one side. "How you doin', Jenny?"

"I'm so sorry about Carol. I'm fine, basically. I guess you're not."

"Right. I'm not."

"Well, why should you be?"

He finally, really, looked at me then, examined me, and gave me a small but genuine smile. "That's nice. Thank you. I really appreciate that. I see already why Carol liked you so much. Everybody else thinks I should be fine. Fucking fine. Like because we were separated, I didn't care about her. Like I wasn't still in love with her. Like I wasn't praying we'd get back together, like it was my idea to divorce to begin with."

"No?"

He shook his head.

"Are you going to sit down?" I asked him.

"I don't know." Steve stood there, clenching his jaw and his fists before he spoke again. "It's hard."

I inhaled a sharp breath of surprise and pity. "Oh, boy, is this the first time since . . . ?"

He nodded and his face started to crumple until he got it under control again.

"Steve, I don't care if you cry. It's okay with me. You can act anyway you want to, really, I don't expect you to make nice just for me."

"Hypocrite," he said.

"What?"

"Who's fighting tears?"

I wiped away the couple he was accusing me of shedding, and then I reached out to grab his black denim jacket sleeve and to tug him over to the sofa that, I supposed, he and Carol had also used as their bed. No wonder he didn't want to sit down there. "Sit with me," I commanded. I felt as if I'd known him forever, as if I could push him around, boss him, scold him, comfort him. All this for a man I'd met only at dinner in some generic convention hotel in some forgotten city in some year I couldn't even remember. "Tell me what's in the envelope. Is that what you said's for me?"

He sat down heavily and began to open the envelope.

What he tugged out looked to me like a small photo album and a single loose photograph. He hesitated, and then he laid it face up gently in my lap. It was Carol and me. Las Vegas. A convention. Two grinning ninnies. The tall happy blond one was me, the tall happy dark one was Carol. Our arms around each other. Slot machines in the background. Dressed to kill for a night at the shows. I already knew what I looked like, but I wanted to drill the memory of her into my mind, and so I raised the photo and stared hard: brown hair to her shoulders; a fresh perm, giving her a bouncy look; big dark eyes with a seriousness in their depths that somewhat belied the laughter around her mouth; thinnish, as befitted a regular runner;

healthy complexion, smooth as powder. The woman in the photograph looked as if she were intelligent, sensitive, quick-witted, lots of fun. She was.

I cleared my throat. "Is this for me?"

"Yeah, sort of."

"Thanks." I looked at him. "Sort of?"

"This album's for you to take, too."

I received it, opened it, saw what it was, and immediately attempted to shove it back at him. "Steve, no, I don't want this, you should keep it." It was an album of pictures of Carol as a child, looking as if it spanned the years from about seven to ten.

"It's not for you to keep," he said. "It's for you to take."

"What's the difference?"

"Listen," he said, bounding to his feet again, leaving me holding all the photographs. "You had lunch? I know a great place, let me take you there. Or you take me." Steve laughed a little. "I'm the impoverished musician. I'm the poor schmuck what's gonna have his late wife's estate held up in probate because my lovin' in-laws don't want me to have the money. It's Thai."

"The restaurant?"

"You're quick. No, what did you think I meant, my in-laws? There are very few Jews from Thailand. We can walk. You'll need to put on different shoes than those things you got on." He was referring to my best black business pumps, which had two-and-a-half-inch heels. "It's not *that* close. You like Thai?"

"Nothing's close," I observed, "when I'm walking in high heels on pavement. Yes, I like Thai. And Pakistani and Cuban and Mongolian and Sengalese and any other ethnic group we don't get at home. There are about as many recent immigrants in Port Frederick as there are Jews in Thailand."

"You eat a lot of white bread up there?"

"We are a lot of white bread." I hesitated, because he was staring at my shoes. "I'll change them, I promise."

"They say when she was trying to fight him off, she made her own footprints. On the sidewalk. In her own blood."

"Oh, my God, Steve, I'm so sorry . . ."

He jerked his gaze away from my feet and turned in a circle, staring at the room around us. His face twisted into a furious expression. "Look at this place! You'd think she was still here! Her parents? You know? They refused to come over and clean out her stuff. Not her clothes, not her office, nothing. I took my stuff when we separated. So they just leave everything as it was"—he indicated the contents of the beautiful rooms with an angry, dismissive wave of his right hand—"like it's a message to me. Like I'm supposed to finally see this, and my guilt is supposed to stab me"—he feigned a knife to his heart—"and I'm supposed to collapse and confess that I did it."

"They think *you* did it?"

He suddenly did appear to collapse, so that he looked like a pitiful, abandoned teddy bear, and so when he looked at me with teary eyes and he said like a sad little boy, "Can I please have a hug?" I did the only thing that felt natural at the time: I quickly crossed the length of the living room to give him one. Carol's husband cried on my shoulder while I patted his back, and then he sniffed and blew his nose while I changed into some tennis shoes. I slipped my business shoes into my brief case (like a good New York executive), and I put an arm around Steve to urge him toward the door.

"What's this?" I said just outside my door.

On the floor lay a pretty little foil-wrapped package tied with pink ribbon. I quickly undid it and discovered a perfect miniature loaf of what looked and smelled like deliciously tart zucchini bread.

"Ah," whispered Steve, "the Mad Baker strikes again!"

I inclined my head toward Mrs. Golding's door, and Steve nodded in confirmation and whispered, "Yeah, we got little gifts like that all the time." He patted his flat abdomen. "I had to move out so I wouldn't gain weight." He raised his voice to the closed door. "*Hi, Mrs. Golding!*"

"Steve, you didn't have a basket of food sent to me, did you?"

"Sure." He was stuffing his handkerchief back into his jeans pocket, but he stopped long enough to offer me a grin that told me he was only kidding. "What was in it? I forget what I ordered."

"Sure." I raised my voice and spoke to the door of 5B. "*Thank you, Mrs. Golding!*"

Steve laughed quietly and said, "You catch on quick."

I rewrapped the bread and slipped back into the apartment to put his latest gift into the wicker basket in the refrigerator. "Thanks, Ida," I murmured. "You sweetheart."

On the way down the stairs, as we walked past the door of 2C, I nudged Steve's arm and inclined my head inquisitively again. And again, he nodded as if he knew exactly what I was talking about, only this time he silently raised the forefinger of his right hand to his temple and made rotating motions with it. Crazy, he was indicating. The resident of 2C was definitely nuts. And then Steve pressed his fingers together and arched them so his right hand looked like a diver poised to spring; he made an actual diving motion with it and looked at me for confirmation. I nodded and whispered, "Jed saved her." Steve leaned toward my ear to whisper into it, "It's a nuthouse. You'll get used to it."

"I don't think so," I whispered back.

5

S TEVE WALKED ME TO A SWEET LITTLE THAI RESTAURANT on
Amsterdam Avenue, where the walls were hung with paintings
of beatifically smiling women and the napkins and tablecloths
were all constructed out of a delicate orchid-tinted paper. We
would have been the only customers were it not for two young
white men seated at a table in a bay whose three long windows
were open; a breeze whistled lightly through the screenless
apertures, rustling the lavender paper on our laps and the orchid edges of our tablecloth. There was a soft fragrance of curry
in the room and a soft tingling of tiny cymbals from an overhead
chime, and with the music of the wind playing with the paper,
it felt like dining in the middle of a Far Eastern bazaar.

"This," I said, "is why I love this city."

He looked around as if he'd never seen it before. "How's
that?"

"You don't have to have a passport to leave home."

Over an appetizer of taro nest, which looked like orange
French fries and tasted like crisp slices of sweet yam, Steve
complained bitterly about Carol's parents.

"They have this crazy idea," he said, not exactly looking at
me.

I dunked a chunk of taro into a tiny white porcelain bowl of sweet plum sauce and raised my eyebrows at him in what I hoped was both an encouraging and a nonjudgmental way.

"Too spicy for you?" he asked.

I lowered my eyebrows. "No, it's perfect. What's their idea?"

"Did you ever meet them?"

I shook my head, my mouth being full.

"Evelyn and Martin." He said it mockingly in highfalutin tones, as if making fun of the rich and proper. "They live in Brooklyn Heights. Sainted Brooklyn, natural home of God's favorite children. I don't think they ever leave it, I don't think they have an idea there is any other world outside of it. I think Evelyn orders all their clothes and furniture, hell, she probably orders their *cars* from catalogs, so they never have to leave the neighborhood. Marty's retired, so he never has to go anyplace but the corner deli and the synagogue. So they don't know how the world works, you get it?"

"Is it germane?"

"No, it's German. Of course, it explains them! And now I'm explaining them to you. So their darling child, their sweet princess, meets this pork-eating Jew musician from the Village, and they freak. And I marry her, and they freak louder. And Carol and me, we get that apartment, here on the Upper West Side, which isn't the Upper East Side and even worse, it isn't Brooklyn. And then we separate, which freaks them out the worst, which is crazy, of course. I mean, you'd think they'd be delighted to lose me, wouldn't you?"

I nodded obligingly.

"But no, they think divorce is awful and it's all my fault. Well, that goes without saying to their way of thinking, although it doesn't stop them from saying it. Again and again. And then Carol goes and gets herself stabbed to death."

He abruptly halted his emotional narrative, long enough to drain his water glass and for his flushed face to return to a more normal shade of muted pink. He hadn't eaten any of the pretty soup in front of him.

I asked quietly, "Is that supposed to be your fault, too?"

"How'd you guess? I made it possible, they said, I provided the"—he again affected an arch tone as if imitating someone, his mother- or father-in-law, I gathered—"the *matrix*, the environment, the potentia*l*ity, because if I hadn't moved out, which *Carol* asked me to do, by the way, it wouldn't have happened."

"Why not?"

"Because she used to run in the mornings, but after I moved out, she started running at night, because that's when we used to walk in the park together or shop or go out to eat or something. It was our time, especially if I had a gig to play later in the evening. After I left, she said it made her feel lonely to be in the apartment at night by herself, and she missed me and she didn't want to. Isn't that a hell of thing to say?"

He stabbed the plate of chicken and crisp noodles in gravy that the waitress set down in front of him and talked angrily to the food. "It's not my fault! She's the one who kicked me out! But try telling that to Evelyn and Marty."

Oddly, when he said that he glanced up at me in a distinctly evaluative sort of way. What was that look about, I wondered? I knew there'd be at least one other side to this story and that Carol's possibly long-suffering parents could probably give me an earful. Fortunately, I'd never have to endure that.

"So what I'd like you to do," Steve said, "is talk to them."

He calmly slopped up a forkful of chicken and gravy.

I stared at him. "And *this* is why we're having lunch."

"No, we're having lunch because I like you and you like me and we're hungry. I can ask you this favor that I wouldn't ask anybody else."

"I hardly know you."

"A while ago, you hugged me like a friend."

"That was my evil twin. And this, I guess, is yours."

"So all you have to do is to go out to Brooklyn, home of the brave, visit E & M, and tell them my side of it. First, you show them the photo of you and Carol to prove what good friends you were, then you give them the album to show them my swell intentions, and then you explain to them that I loved their daughter, I didn't kill her."

"I also don't know *them*, Steve! They've just lost their daughter in a horrible and tragic way, and I am not, absolutely not, going to intrude on them. Forget it, just unequivocally forget it."

"Your husband's a cop, right?"

I nodded warily. I detected a list here, and this was the

second item on it. No, the third. First, lunch, then the in-laws, and now Geof. How long was this list going to be anyway?

"I would also appreciate it if you will ask him to goose the cops down here. I don't think they're doing diddlysquat. No suspects. No leads, they claim. But they talk to my in-laws night and day, and they're beginning to look at me funny. I think they'd get their asses in gear and find the real killer if your husband poked 'em a time or two, okay?"

"Steve—"

"Don't use that fucking gentle tone with me, I know what *that* means, it means—"

"Right, get real. You're dreaming if you think that Manhattan cops are going to do one thing differently just because some cop from some hick town they never heard of asks them to. No way. And, two, anonymous street attacks are practically impossible to solve unless a witness comes forward or somebody confesses. My guess is that happens in this town about as often as you eat bologna on white bread with mayo."

"Gross. But ask him, see what he says."

"All right, I'll talk to my husband, but I will not play shuttle diplomacy for you with your in-laws."

"And you call yourself a friend."

"What happened, Steve, between you two?"

He shrugged and then warbled off-key, "Two different worlds, we lived in two different worlds . . ." Oh dear, I thought, if Steve was hoping to make it as a singer, he'd better keep his day job. As he apparently didn't *have* a day job, that could be a problem. "I wear jeans and smoke dope and play keyboard in bars at night, she wore suits to offices during the day and didn't even drink wine, and those sorts of differences can give you a lot to argue about." He changed the subject quickly. "So where do you go from here, Jenny?"

"Downtown to meet with Pat Vinitsky."

"Patty-Cakes? Give her my love. Come on, I'll walk you to the subway."

"No, I'm taking a cab."

"Don't waste the money. You can take the subway right out here for a tenth of what it would cost you to—"

"I don't care. I'm not going on a New York subway. Vinitsky said this was all expenses paid, but even if I have to pay for it myself, I am only taking cabs. Your subways are smelly, dirty, and dangerous. Given a choice in life, why would I want to go underground when I could stay above ground where it's—"

"Smelly, dirty, and dangerous?"

"Interesting, bright, and sunny."

"Oh, you tourists. Won't you even go on one with me?"

"Not with you, not with anybody."

"That's ridiculous."

"Fine, it's ridiculous, but call me a cab, anyway."

"It would be more appropriate to call you a moron. Carol, you will note, did not die on the subway. I'll bet she took the subway every day, but she never once died there. Not once. Never once got stabbed there or robbed or assaulted in any way, unless you count aggressive beggars. No, she died aboveground on a day when it was sunny and bright. And interesting. Fuck, yes, what an interesting day *that* was in New York City. But, hey, you think it's safer up here with the majority of the rapists and murderers, fine, hang out where you like, just like Carol—"

"Steve?"

He was flushing, angry, but he caught himself on the tone of my voice. "Sorry. But there you go again, using that sympathetic voice on me again. You're going to make me cry again, Jenny Cain, and you know what happens to grown men who care caught crying in public in this city?"

"No, what?"

"They get a lot of women that way."

I threw my napkin at him. And then I noticed that our little waitress was standing by the bay window rubbing her hands together and looking distressed. The table there was empty. The breeze blowing in through the trio of open windows flapped an edge of the orchid tablecloth up onto the table. When she saw me looking, she gestured to where the two men had been seated and then to the windows. "Steve," I said, unbelieving, "did what I think just happen really happen?"

"Yeah, they skipped on the bill."

"Out the *window?*"

"Why not?"

I stared at him, shocked.

He grinned wickedly at me. "Oh, you're such a tourist. Listen, things happen in this city that don't happen in nicer places. Strangers do things to other strangers that they might not do to each other in your sweet little hometown. They walk out on restaurant bills. They beat each other up. They kill each other—"

He stopped. Took a deep, shaky breath. Pushed back from the table and stood up. "Come on, Jenny. Pay the damn bill, and let's split." As I watched the back of his black denim as he stalked out of the restaurant, leaving me to pick up the tab, a nasty thought entered my mind: Was that his attitude toward his marriage to Carol . . . to let her pay the bills . . . and then to split? Now, if his in-laws dropped their accusations, he'd have plenty of money to pay any bills. There was something else, too: Although it was sometimes difficult to remember, considering how many people I knew who smoked it, marijuana was still illegal in this country. And Carol had said that somebody she knew was doing something illegal. No, surely, that wasn't it, because in the first place, it was a pretty minor offense, and in the second place, what harm could his habit be doing to other people?

I stopped beside the cash register.

Unless Steve was doing more than smoking it?

I paid and followed him but slowly, trying to locate a pleasant, unsuspicious expression to paste back on my face again.

6

AMSTERDAM AVENUE WAS ONE-WAY GOING NORTH . . . so Steve walked me across an intersection to catch a cab going east . . . so that I might eventually go south . . . without having to pay extra to drive around a block or two or three . . . depending on street construction or parades or demonstrations or . . . you never knew.

"I always forget," I said to him, "how in New York it's either amazingly easy to get somewhere or supremely difficult for the same destination from the same starting point on the same day."

"It's the city where you can't get there from here," he agreed.

There was an adorable elderly couple walking in front of us as we stepped off the curb. I nudged Steve's arm, and we smiled at each other in the complicity of our warm feelings for the pair. They were white-haired, and he was nearly bald, with liver spots showing through on his sweet, fuzzy skull. They must have been in their late eighties, both of them shorter than us. Her frail left arm was sweetly entwined with his thin right one, and she also leaned lightly on a silver cane. The old man led her carefully, slowly, tenderly, across the intersection. Steve and I backed off our own pace in order to watch them and to keep from overrunning them.

Just ahead of the old couple, a white van nosed a foot or so into the crosswalk, so that the little pair had to step a couple of inches out of their way to thread around it.

The sweet little old man turned around, shook his tiny fist at the driver of the van, and yelled, *"Asshole!"*

The driver, a young man, leaned out his window and shouted back, *"Fuck you!"*

"You're not man enough!"

"Motherfucker!"

Steve and I picked up our pace and skirted the old couple, making it to the other side of the intersection before the light changed. I looked back. The white van had plowed on, though the young driver was still looking back and yelling, while the old couple continued their slow pace in the crosswalk, with dozens of vehicles backed up, waiting for them.

I looked at Steve, and we burst out laughing.

"What did I tell you about this city?" he said. "I even fall for it sometimes. I was watching that old man and that old lady and I was starting to get all sentimental, you know? How that could have been Carol and me when we got old, you know? And then he turns around and gives that driver hell!"

"Which you will do at his age," I pointed out.

"Damn right," he said as he flagged down a cab for me.

This, I decided, was not a quaint little tourist story I would tell my husband when I spoke to him that evening.

"I'll call you!" Steve yelled from the sidewalk as my cab took off. "After you talk to M & E!"

Martin and Evelyn? I thought as I waved back. *Don't wait up.*

While in the back seat of the cab, I changed back into my business heels and then reshuffled the tennis shoes into my briefcase, which was then not easy to snap shut. I began to grasp why so many New York women carried backpacks, even over their suits. Funny, it seemed to me, to don a backpack to go into a city, but then what did I know about roughing it? Some people, like my husband, would term New York City a "wilderness adventure," complete with snakes, tigers, and things that went bump in the night.

BUT I WOULDN'T WANT TO *DIE* THERE

The ride to Pat Vinitsky's office took longer than I expected, because we traveled south to the financial district by way of a slight detour: the Upper East Side.

My cab driver appeared to speak only two words of English: *hello* and *yes,* the latter delivered with a certain diabolical hissing emphasis: yissss. I gave him the address, which I believed to be near the World Trade Center, which I made the mistake of assuming that anybody could find, if by no other means than by simply sticking one's head out the window and looking up. He said yisss. I gave him the cross streets, as well; he said yisss. I said, when I had a feeling we were heading east when we should have been going south, did he know where it was, and he assured me yisss. I inquired if he had a map, and he said yissss but never did produce one. I fumbled for my own, but then I had trouble catching the names of the streets as we lurched and whizzed by the street signs. I suggested he ask somebody, and he agreed yisss but didn't seem to have a radio with which to call anybody. I said, let me out here, wherever that is, which looked a lot like the United Nations to me. Yisss, he said and pointed to the eight dollars and forty-five cents on his meter. Nooo, I said, handed him a five, and heaved myself out of his cab while he shouted at me, using all sorts of words, none of which was hello or yes.

I scooted down a side street that was one-way going the way he couldn't turn, and then I hiked up another street, where I hailed another cab.

"Hello!" said the driver.

I was hot, sweaty, angry, and afraid I'd be late.

"Hello, *what?*" I demanded.

"Hello, madam?" he offered. "Hello, sugarplum? Hello, my baby, hello, my honey, hello, my ragtime doll? Hello, hello, where the hello do you want to go?"

I told him.

We went.

Not only was I not late, but I still had time to kill before I was due to ascend the heights to see Vinitsky. I decided to get my nails done at one of the incredibly cheap manicure joints that seemed to sprout like hangnails on every street and corner. They lacquered me a glowing mauve and put me under a tiny pink fan to dry quickly. Did Carol do this, too, I wondered, did she have some favorite little manicure shop? I remembered that her nails always looked beautiful, but she claimed she only put on polish for conventions. Did she like the Thai restaurant where Steve had taken me? Would she have ordered the taro nest? I would have bet so; when she and I dined together at conventions, we always got a laugh when we ordered exactly the same things, laughed at the same things, got ticked off at the same things.

My half hour in the nail shop gave me time to remember Carol in more detail—her great laugh, how easily she could be moved to tears, how she had claimed to feel like a fish out of water any place outside of this city. It also afforded me a chance to relax for a few moments from the frenetic New York pace that buzzed like a high-voltage transformer just outside.

Inside, all was hot pink and feminine, a warm little womb.

Since none of the manicurists spoke English, I didn't even have to talk to anyone, only point to the color I wanted applied to my nails. And smile my thanks as I left a tip. And sigh in relief, because in here, if anybody was calling anybody else names, I couldn't understand them . . . and nobody could jump out a window to maim or kill themselves, because we were on the first floor . . . and because here, whatever got Carol couldn't get me. At least here, I felt safe in the big city.

7

I'LL FILL YOU IN ON THE HART FOUNDATION."

Patricia Vinitsky reminded me of the nonfilter cigarettes I smoked for one semester in college: short, quick, lethally direct. She wore a power suit, black, natch, with the jacket slung over the back of her upholstered desk chair. Short, tight black skirt. Tight black silk blouse buttoned to the top of its Mandarin collar. Power high heels, black. Big-time gold earrings. Power haircut clipped razor short. No doubt it did not so much as stir in the wind when she put the top down on her black BMW convertible.

Whoa, Jenny, I chided myself, *it hasn't been easy for this woman to get here, in this office, with this view. And who else is wearing all-black in this office?*

"Great view," I said.

She glanced over her shoulder dismissively: So much for the forty-four most valuable acres of real estate in the world.

"I'm impressed," I insisted.

"Yeah, but consider the source," she said deadpan.

I stared, then burst out laughing, and she smiled back at me.

"It looks like a pop-up card in a Hallmark store," I said.

"Yeah. We fold it up when we go home."

Her porcelain fingernails were painted a deep burgundy,

41

which was her only color apart from the reddish black dye in her hair. She had incongruously soft, round, pale cheeks. They looked pinchable, as men had no doubt tested to their extreme and immediate regret. Patty Vinitsky looked as if she'd tolerate cheek-pinchers about as well as I'd put up with fanny-patters. She looked as if she didn't give a damn if anybody ever liked her, but I did because of those two jokes. I seemed to be liking everybody that day; who knew, I might even have grown fond of that yisssing taxi driver, as much time as it had looked as if we'd be spending in each other's company.

Vinitsky clicked her gold pen constantly as she talked. She paced. She crossed and recrossed her short, thin legs when she sat on the edge of her desk. She jiggled a shoe loose and dangled it from her toes. She ran her hands through her hair, what there was of it, which was about as much as your average Marine recruit. I had to keep swiveling to follow her, as she maintained perpetual motion.

"The Hart Foundation was founded in 1959 by Emiline Hart whose father, Richard, made his loot in the textile industry. She was his only child. Never married. No kids. A recluse, bit of an eccentric. One of those crazy lady types who live in near-poverty, and then you find a billion bucks stashed in cash in a shoe box. Only in Emiline's case, it was six mil in blue chips and bonds, and she kept the certificates in a cookie jar. There was a certain logic to it, I guess."

"Blue chip and chocolate chip?" I guessed.

Her half grin was approving, apologetic. I liked her even better.

"So she directed all of that money into a foundation with instructions that it benefit charities in this city, and she named it after herself. That pleases me, because so many women, especially of earlier generations, wouldn't and won't do that." Vinitsky suddenly faked a fluted voice and fluttered her porcelain fingernails like a Victorian maiden. "Oh, don't name it after *me*, little ol' nobody me! Name it for my illustrious father or my wonderful husband or my swell son, but not after *me*, little old invisible, useless, self-deprecating, female me!" I laughed appreciatively, but she didn't pause to acknowledge the applause. "We're like a small country here in New York, with a big population—or a whole lot of small countries with smaller populations, depending on how you want to look at it—so that leaves us lots of leeway in how we spend the money. We don't have any special 'cause.' We fund the arts. Social services. Medicine. Whatever. You apply for it, we'll consider it."

"Sounds like the foundation I worked for."

"Yeah." She looked up at me sharply. "What happened there?"

"I'll tell you sometime when you have a couple of days."

"Why not now?"

"I don't have to. I'm not applying for the job."

She gave me a cadgy look. "Yet?"

"Yet."

"You will. You'll like it. Assuming you enjoy crisis, but you must or you wouldn't be a foundation director. We have emergencies right now, Jen, and I'm counting on you to turn them into business-as-usual."

"Yes, ma'am."

I half-saluted; she half-grinned.

"Carol got us into them, and you're going to get us out. Not that she wasn't great—she was, believe me—but things were falling apart toward the end, I mean, that is, for a while before she died. A couple of times I could have gladly killed her myself over a couple of things. If I didn't know better, I'd say she killed herself to avoid our next board meeting." Vinitsky laughed, but then a quick glance at my face must have told her she was treading narrowly close to the edge of actually offending me. "Hell, it was no wonder she couldn't concentrate, her personal life was a mess, going through a divorce and all. He's a bum. She should have left him a long time ago, like about two minutes after they met. I was handling the divorce for her, by the way, so don't look at me as if I don't know. I know what kind of man Steve Wolff is."

"What is he?"

"Selfish, lazy, greedy."

"What every wife says about the man she's divorcing?"

She shrugged and smiled a little. "Okay, maybe. Now the bum gets the money. Ain't life interesting?"

"I had lunch with Steve. He sent his love."

"I'll bet he did. Return to sender."

"What did you mean about the board meeting, Pat? Are you

saying that if Carol had lived, she would have been in trouble with the directors?"

"Let me put it this way, Jenny: If one of the directors had made a motion to fire her, I would have jiggled somebody's arm to get him to second it. Just to get the discussion going, if nothing else. I don't know if I'd have actually lobbied to can her, but there was cause."

"Like what?"

"Take out a pen and make a list, because the causes of Carol's problems with our board are also the emergencies you're going to unmess. I believe I alluded to them when we talked on the phone. Number one. Thanks to Carol, God rest her soul, we've got us a reluctant donor. You know the type?"

"I do."

"This one's a woman by the name of Marguerite Stewart. Richer than fudge torte. We had her baited, hooked, and ready to reel, she was so close to signing a charitable remainder trust with us that we could practically see the ink dripping from her pen. It was earmarked for the rehabilitation of ex-convicts, because that's her son's favorite cause. He's a minister. They run a halfway house; in fact, it's *her* house, they all live in it, just a happy little family of former felons. But then out of the blue, she backed out, and she specifically and particularly said that she didn't want anything more to do, ever in her life, with Carol Margolis."

I didn't take this quite as dramatically as Vinitsky presented it, as I knew from experience that foundation donors could be mighty touchy folks. They could embrace you one day and then the very next day they could get their feelings so hurt over a real or imagined slight that they'd threaten to cut off the money. To spite *your* face. Neither did she need to explain to me that a charitable remainder trust was one that was established by a donor with the idea of paying income to a beneficiary, such as a spouse, until that person died, leaving all of the remaining assets to a foundation. So I inquired calmly, as befitted the issue, "How did Carol offend your donor?"

"I don't know, but you're going to find out. You are going to stroke Mrs. Stewart's feathers until they're so smooth the money just slides out from under them. She lives in Brooklyn, just off Flatbush. Call her, convince her to see you, make sure she understands that you're not Carol, maybe that will make a difference."

"Why would she think I was Carol?"

Vinitsky shrugged. "I don't think she's quite with it, or else why would she act this way? I wouldn't call her *non compos,* but I wouldn't say she's fully *compos* either."

"Can you tell me any more than that?"

"Check the files at Carol's office."

"In her apartment?"

"Yes. I admired her for that, you know. Her insistence that we shouldn't rent an office for her, that we could just pay a portion of her mortgage, and she'd work out of her home. Saved us a bunch. Carol was careful with the foundation's money, at least when it came to spending it on herself. Lately, she was finding other ways to lose it, however."

"Like the case of Mrs. Stewart?"

"Yes. And like the case of one Mr. Damon Calendar, who is driving me personally crazy. He's the manager of the Upstage Theater, an amateur outfit in the Village. We agreed to fund it in quarterly installments. Carol didn't get the third check to them when it was due, before she died, and now Calendar is raising hell, calling me all the time to *demand*—if you can believe it—the check. He says they'll fold before the second performance of their next production if we don't pay them immediately. Actually, I believe him. These little theater groups are always at death's door. I don't know what the hell delayed Carol, because she was usually efficient about disbursements." The cynical look in her eyes deepened. "Maybe she couldn't stand to see another production of *King Lear,* maybe she thought the world has seen enough of *King Lear* to last a millenium. So you check it out. Get him the money, get the jerk off my back."

"How do I reach Calendar?"

"Files in her office."

I mimicked her efficiency: "Next?"

She grinned. "Everybody's pissed off. Lucky you. Next you've got another donor, two of them really, husband and wife by the names of Dorothy and Malcolm Lloyd. Black couple. I mention that only because the point is that they've been active in civil rights since the forties. They established a donor-advised field of interest fund to serve minorities. Well, they advised us, all right, and our committee went against their wishes—"

"Which is their legal right to do," I interjected.

"Of course. And the donors were adequately advised of that by us and by their own attorneys before they signed anything. Try telling them that now, however! Now they're really ticked. Dr. Lloyd is threatening to bust the trust, and he may be mad enough to do it this time by the simple expedient of forcing us to pay so much money in legal fees to defend the damned thing that we just give up."

"*This* time?"

"Choleric, our Malcolm is."

"High blood pressure?"

"That's Dorothy's excuse for him. Spoiled is my diagnosis of the good doctor. Spoiled by Dorothy, by the fact that he used to be a surgeon, and you know how they can be, and probably by his doting mommy and grandmother in their time."

"And you want me to calm him down?"

"Talk to him, tell him blah blah blah, whatever it takes."

"Blah blah? Can you be more specific?"

"Yeah, I can specifically advise you to charm Dorothy, as she's slightly more reasonable than he is and probably the one person in the world with a hope of managing him."

Donor-advised field of interest funds were interesting creatures, frequently established by well-intentioned folks who wanted to control things without giving that appearance.

"What did they want you to fund, Pat?"

"The Black Company."

"Ah, yes," I said.

"I see you know how controversial it is."

"We have newspapers, yes."

"No kidding? Even newspapers? Next thing you'll be telling me you have telephones and running water up there. Well, I suppose you don't have to hang out at the Russian Tea Room to hear the word about the Black Company. You know the leaders are suspected of graft on a colossal scale. When we set up the fund, the Lloyds didn't tell us *that* was the minority interest they wanted to serve! Now Dr. Lloyd refuses to withdraw his support. He still wants us to channel the money to them. He says they're doing the job that needs to be done, funding small businesses in black communities where no other money will go, and that all this controversy is just more white opposition to black progress."

"But your board declined tactfully."

She nodded her confirmation.

"Where are you putting the money instead?"

This time her smile was genuine, with no hint of cynicism attached to it. "To a really wonderful gardening project in a basically black neighborhood."

"Basically black?"

"Yeah, I know it makes it sound like a dinner dress. But it's on the lower edge of the South Bronx, and most of the neighborhood is comprised of people of color, and most of those shades are at the darker end of the spectrum. We think it has the potential to launch several small businesses itself. And don't think our committee is like an all-white jury passing judgment on a black victim either. No way. We've got so many colors and flavors on our board we could pass for Baskin-Robbins. I'm about as close to a traditional WASP as we get, and I'm a Polish Catholic with ovaries. But Dr. Lloyd disagrees vehemently with our decision. I might even say that he disagrees violently, considering the fact that he threw a notebook at Carol the last time she tried to talk to him. He won't listen, not to anybody, except you."

"Me? Why me?"

"Because you're our last hope. Because I have faith in you, because Carol did, and because you come recommended by half the foundation community in this country. If you pull this one off, I'll approve your request for taxi fare if I have to pull the money out of the pockets of my board members. What do you have against our lovely subway system anyhow?"

"I want to live," I said.

"In this town? Good luck! Now, one more thing." The gold pen clicked like crazy as I poised my own pen to take down more notes. "There's one more crisis, a project, really terrific, that has to be approved like yesterday, so we can get money to them like tomorrow. It's run by a dynamo by the name of Andrei Bolen, a Frenchman with a passion for literacy. The project's called Book'Em, and it's in Harlem. Its objective is to get the kids out of jail and into the libraries."

"In this city? Good luck!"

But she didn't laugh at my sally. She seemed more intense about this item on my agenda, more personally involved. "Carol was supposed to approve it, but she died first." That was spoken in such an impatient tone of voice that I was tempted to mutter, *Why, how terribly inconsiderate of her.*

"Go up there—"

"To Harlem? Listen, I'm just a small-town white girl."

"Talk to Andrei—it's only a formality—fill out the papers, get them to me, and I'll ram them through the board by phone and fiat. I want this done, got it?"

"I'll look it over," I said.

She paused to give me an appraising glance. She, no dummy, knew that my careful words meant that I wouldn't agree to rubber-stamp any applicant.

"All right, that's it." She swung down off her desk, clearly ready to bring this interview to a close. "Those are the fires you have to put out. Call me when you douse them. But save it for the end of the day. This is *pro bono* work for me, and I've got a shitload of paying clients to pamper. Okay, you think you got everything you need? No, wait, there's one more thing."

I looked up at her expectantly.

"Carol's parents, Mr. and Mrs. Margolis. They want to meet you."

My heart sank. What could I possibly say to grieving strangers except that I had loved their daughter and I was terribly sorry she'd been murdered? *Well,* I thought in resignation, *okay, I guess that's what I could say to them.*

Vinitsky handed me a piece of paper with their names and a phone number and address. "They're expecting you this afternoon. Any time you show up. I don't think they go out much. Do this first."

"Can I take a cab?"

"You could, but—" She got a funny look on her face and turned to glance out her windows and then back at me. "Have you ever been to Brooklyn? No? I grew up there. Wonderful place. Look, it's a gorgeous day. Sunny, not much wind. You won't have time for much business the rest of the day, so don't take a cab. I'll tell you what to do for your first trip into Brooklyn: walk across the bridge."

"The bridge?"

"The Brooklyn Bridge."

"I don't think—"

"Yes, do it. You'll be glad. It's safe and beautiful. Come here." She raised the slatted blinds at one of her windows while I walked over to stand beside her. Together, we looked out at a magnificent view that included several bridges. "That's it." She pointed to a gorgeous suspension edifice, erected on the top of two gigantic gothic towers, which spanned a narrow section of the East River. "Really, you gotta walk it. Weather's perfect, you don't even have to take a cab to get there, and Mr. and Mrs. Margolis live within walking distance on the other side. I love that bridge, we all love it. It's a great experience, especially if you've never done it before. You won't believe the view. Got a map?"

Feeling intimidated by her idea, I went back to my briefcase to dig out my map. She applied her gold pen to it. "See this green space?" She used her pen to point to an actual green space forty stories below us. "There it is, right down there. That's City Hall Park. Just walk onto the bridge from there. Couldn't be simpler. When you get across . . ." She penned in a route on my map. "You'll love it. You'll call me and tell me it was a veritable epiphany of an experience." She put away her pen and stuck out her right hand. "But don't call me until after five o'clock, not unless you get mugged or raped or something."

"Thanks a lot."

"Well," she smiled, "you'll need a lawyer."

"Any other advice, Pat?"

As she walked me toward the door, she said, "Yeah. Don't run in a park after dark, don't take the A train past 86th Street, don't expect to find a cab about the time the theater lets out, don't wear shoes when you live in an apartment with a wood floor, and never get your nails done at one of those cheap joints, 'cause some of 'em never wash their equipment, and you get a fungus that makes your nails turn black and fall off, and they don't grow back for a whole year. That's about it. Other than that, you're on your own."

Her phone rang, so she probably didn't notice the look of horror on my face as my newly painted fingernails cut moons over Manhattan into my palms. Was it my imagination or were they turning a little dark under the mauve?

As I let myself out, I noticed a plaque hanging beside her law degree. It was attributed to John A. Roebling, "Architect of the Brooklyn Bridge," and it said: "The hero is admired and proclaimed a public benefactor. But nobody knows . . . who can hide me from myself?"

I took one last look at Pat Vinitsky, busy on the phone. What did she want to hide from others or from herself?

It sounded to me as if half of New York had been angry at my friend Carol at the time she died, including her boss and her husband. All of the people Vinitsky had described to me were "do-gooders" of the sort Carol had probably meant in her phone message to me. Had Carol reported one of the foundation clients for some abuse? Or had they "stopped" her before she had a chance to turn them in? Were any of those "charitable" people angry enough to kill her?

Those were the questions I asked myself as I stood near City Hall Park, trying to decide how to get across the river to Brooklyn.

I'll go slowly, I decided, meaning that I would move quietly and deliberately toward my goal of connecting Carol's message with her murder. *I'll take my time, feel for impressions, just let people talk and maybe give them an opportunity to hang themselves, and I'll refrain from asking pointed questions that might alarm anybody. I am not a cop. So I'll be what I am: Carol's friend, the new kid on the job.* For good measure, I added to my vow: *And I will also entertain the notion that I might just possibly be wrong about this whole business and that maybe she really was killed by a mugger.*

The bridge stretched far into the distance.

"The hell with walking."

I took a cab to Brooklyn.

"I'm very intelligent," the cabbie informed me straight off.

How do you reply to a statement like that? "Really?" seemed

to imply doubt on my part; "How nice for you," sounded condescending; "I'd never guess by looking at you," was not the ticket; and "Do tell," offered the awful chance that he might.

"Me, too," I said.

We drove onto the bridge in the companionable silence of peers.

8

T HE TAXI PULLED UP IN FRONT OF A GRACEFUL OLD HIGH-
stoop brownstone rowhouse on Columbia Heights. *What is
brownstone anyway,* I wondered? I decided to test the cabbie
to see if he knew as much as he claimed.

"What is brownstone anyway?"

"A form of sandstone. It's only used for facades, because it's
too weak to use for building blocks."

"Who killed Carol Margolis?"

He turned his head quickly. "What'd ya say?"

"Nothing." I paid him, adding a good tip. "Thanks."

The dark stone was a gorgeous backdrop for the trees that
were starting to bud out and for the red tulips lined up against
black wrought iron fences. I glimpsed the river and a promenade through a gap between buildings and decided to find my
way back there to take a few minutes to gather my emotions and
my thoughts before climbing the stairs to see Carol's parents.

A promenade it was, with a wonderfully long and wide foot-
path made of paving stones and a panoramic view of Manhattan
all the way from the Statue of Liberty to the Upper East Side.

BUT I WOULDN'T WANT TO *DIE* THERE

I leaned against a railing overlooking a highway and the East
River and took out my map to identify the sights: There was
Governor's Island and Ellis Island to my left, with ferries plying
to and fro; the Battery on the very tip of lower Manhattan; and
the South Street Seaport straight across. Then, as I looked once
more at my map, holding it so the eastern side of Manhattan
was facing me, I made such an astonishingly Freudian discovery
that I had to laugh out loud. Had nobody ever noticed this
before? No wonder New York was such a swaggeringly macho
city: On the map, it was the spitting image of an uncircumcized,
dangling penis, and the Bronx was the scrotum! "I'll be
damned," I laughed to myself. "If this thing ever gets stiff, it'll
fertilize half of New Jersey!"

That thought lightened my mood considerably.

By the time I turned to look once again for the home of
Carol's parents, I thought I could handle the situation. On the
promenade behind the Margolis house, an old man and an old
woman sat close together on a green bench. As I looked for a
way back to the street, the elderly woman said, "Yes?" I wasn't
sure she was talking to me, so I murmured an all-purpose hello
and took another tentative step, looking for a gate.

"May we help you?" she asked.

"I'm trying to get to the home of Evelyn and Martin
Margolis."

The man slowly got to his feet.

"Yes?" he said.

And then it hit me. My God, these "old" people were Carol's
parents, who probably weren't much over sixty, if that. I was
too stunned to speak for a moment, too frightened by their
stooped backs, their weary faces, their infinitely sad expres-
sions. They were holding hands even as he stood to greet me.

"I'm Jenny Cain, Mr. and Mrs. Margolis."

Evelyn Margolis reached out her other hand to me, and I
grasped it tightly, allowing her to pull me down onto the bench
beside her. Her husband sank back to his place.

"I'm so sorry," I said to them.

We didn't speak for awhile. I didn't know what held their
tongues, but respect and nervousness held mine. I awaited a
cue from them. When none came immediately, we just sat
there together gazing out over the river at the tug and barge

traffic, at the setting sun, the bridge, and the skyscrapers as if we'd sat there all of our lives and would remain seated there until our lives ended. Actually, I couldn't really have said what they were looking at; maybe their eyes registered what I saw or maybe they were seeing memories, maybe of Carol—little girl Carol—playing in front of them on the pavement. I was hearing traffic, a few birds, a conversation two benches down, and the sounds of children playing near us. But Mr. and Mrs. Margolis may have been listening for their dead daughter's voice. Just in front of us, a male pigeon, his chest feathers all plumped up into iridescent purples and pinks, vainly (in both senses of the word) attempted to woo a little lady pigeon who kept walking away from him, pecking at the pavement, and who plainly couldn't have cared less. When he finally gave up the pursuit, my heart went out to him—he looked so much like a high school kid who'd just been turned down for a dance, and now he had to make that long walk back across the gym, trying to hold his chest out, with all his buddies and the other girls watching. Maybe he had a bad line, maybe he'd said, "Ey, babe, nice setta chest feathers ya got on ya!"

As if I'd asked her a question, Mrs. Margolis started to talk in a gentle, heartbroken voice.

"We view one another, people do, from our own windows, Jenny, never knowing how the very same sight may appear to other people from their own windows. I look across this river, and I see architecture, specific and beautiful. I see high-rising modern buildings designed by architects I could name for you, because I'm interested in that sort of thing. I don't much think of the people inside of those buildings, but Marty, here, he doesn't see the buildings at all—"

"Well, I see them," he said in a sweet and gently interrupting tone, "but as a sort of block of things. Not like individuals, not like people."

"I see the parts of buildings right away," Mrs. Margolis continued. "Cornices. Mortices. Scrolls and gargoyles. I notice it all, and I either hate it or admire it. But I see it, detail by detail, and I notice the differences between the buildings, and I feast on those differences, some of them, and I mourn others." Her soft voice snagged on the word *mourn*, and she had to back up, getting a running jump, and try it again like a horse at a gate that proved too high the first time. The soft words that appeared to mean nothing, that appeared unrelated to her daughter's death, flowed on, dragging sadness up from my chest and forcing it into my eyes and down my cheeks in a pulsing of tears that I couldn't seem to stop from openly flowing. I dabbed at my face with my free hand while Carol's parents, grown so recently elderly, talked to me about the view across the river. "Marty doesn't notice those details," she said. "Not unless I point them out to him or unless he looks long enough."

She paused, and for a while, there was silence on our bench again, except for the noises of my crying. And then he resumed his part of their duet of longing and loneliness.

"While Evelyn is staring at those damn buildings, I'm thinking about who's working in them. All those millions of people. Maybe every one of them would like to buy a water purifier system from me, like I used to sell before I sold the company. I could go back to work, maybe get all of those businesses that buy bottled water to switch to my system. It just hooks up to the faucet, you know." He glanced at me, saw my tears, tightened his jaw visibly, and wiped his left hand under his nose. Then he looked away but not before putting his wife's hand into his lap and grasping it with his other hand, too. "It's very clean, my water, does a hell of a lot more than just take the chlorine out, that's all some of those cheap systems do, you know, and they gum up, trap bacteria, and make you sick, that's what they can do. I know all this, see, and I know that all those millions of people over there, they don't know that. And I don't just think of them as customers, no, sir, not like they're just wallets and billfolds to me. No, I'm thinking of them as individual people. Like pregnant ladies who should be drinking pure for their babies. And old men, maybe some guy, he's close to retirement, and he could live longer, I do really believe this, drinking pure water, not that junk everybody drinks out of the tap."

"So here we are," his wife said, taking up the chorus, "looking out the same window, so to speak, this window we have on the promenade, on the river and the bridge and the city, but Marty and I are seeing two different views. And it's nice, you know, to share those views. I tell him what he's missing, not seeing the buildings as I do. I tell him about the architects, what I know about them, which maybe isn't all that much, which maybe is only what I know from reading *Life* magazines and old *Architectural Digests*. And he listens and learns some. But he says, how can you just see glass and steel, bricks and stone, and not think of the people inside them. So he tells me what he thinks about the women and men and children."

We had another moment of silence then that lengthened and extended into the twilight. I couldn't have talked if I'd known what to say, as the tears were sliding out of my eyes, down my face, choking my throat.

"Well," Evelyn Margolis said in a shaky voice, "what we mean to say, what we're trying to say is: We look at people from different windows. I saw my daughter one way. My sweet child. My dear girl, smart, oh, she was so smart! And stubborn, that was my child. But Marty, he sees her different, because he's looking at her from a different window."

I felt helpless, almost angry. What did they want from me? Why were they making me sit on that public bench and weep for them?

"Tell her, Marty," Evelyn said. "Tell her how you saw Carol."

"She was my baby," he said, and his voice lowered and quavered with so much pain I didn't think I could bear to hear it, so how could he bear to feel it? "Always my baby. Stubborn? Nah, that was just mother–daughter stuff, that was just Evelyn wanting Carol to do everything like we did. She was sure of herself, that was my girl. Confident, you know? Smart, oh, yes, she was smarter than both of us. And nice? My baby was a nice girl, always a nice girl to her mother and me. My baby." He trailed off, thank God. I couldn't have stood much more of it. But then they hit me with it between the eyes.

"Jenny Cain," her mother pronounced. "Carol talked about you. Her beautiful, blond gentile friend from up in Massachusetts. She said we'd love you, she said we might even confuse you with a Jewish girl." Mrs. Margolis laughed a little. "She knew we'd like that, that's why she said it, to make us laugh, to make us like you. I guess nobody else'd say that about you, because nobody else in the whole world would look at you from the same window that Carol did. That's gone now, that view of you, of us, of the world, that nobody else had. But maybe you can still kind of see Carol from your window. You can tell us what she looked like to you, let us stand at your window with you, so we can see her from another angle, maybe help us to round out her memory, so she's full and complete, and with all of us helping each other, she'll never be forgotten."

They waited for me to begin speaking.

Carol, I thought, *help me with this! Give me the words about yourself to say to your parents.* Maybe it was she who reminded me of the photograph in my briefcase, the one of Carol and me that Steve had given me. I fished it out and handed it to them. It helped; they looked at the photo, then, instead of at me. Mrs. Margolis, with her fingers, stroked the image of her daughter.

"The first time I saw Carol was in New Orleans." I started to add the phrase "I think" but stopped myself from doing it. This wasn't a time to be vague; this was a time to be specific and concrete, so the Margolises would get a really good picture of what I'd seen in their daughter. "I can see her, still, coming down a hall toward me. She was walking with two other people, but I can't recall them. I just remember this vibrant thin woman. Her dark hair, those lively eyes, that bright color to her face when she was happy or angry or excited about something. Red. My God, I do remember, she had on a red dress. Great red dress."

I had to stop at that to take a breath before I could go on.

"I loved the way she laughed, that hilarious giggle that would just get away from her sometimes. She was loud." Lord, had I really said that? I glanced at her parents, afraid I'd offended them, but Mr. Margolis was smiling, remembering. Well, she *was* loud. "A lot louder than I am. Big voice. Big presence for such a slender person. Great jokes. Carol told great jokes. Like . . ." Crazily, I reached back into my brain, trying to come up with one. "Like the one about the little boy who asked his mother if he could have a Coke, and his mother said, 'What are the magic words?' and he said, 'You're thin and beautiful.' Carol told a bunch of us that one night in, I don't know, San Francisco, after we'd all had a couple of drinks, and we were on the floor, laughing. Oh, and I remember how sweet she was to people she didn't know. I mean, to people she knew, too. But I was always struck by how decently she behaved to people like waiters and maids, people who can't afford to be rude to you if you're unpleasant to them. That shows character, and Carol had it."

I couldn't continue; I was exhausted by this effort. "I liked her. No, I loved her. I feel so bad for you. I'll write you a letter, and I'll try to remember everything I ever heard her say or do and how she looked to me, everything, and I'll send it to you."

Mrs. Margolis handed the photo back to me.

"Carol had nice friends," she said, making me feel blessed.

We shared a different kind of quiet then, as if something important had been released into the crisp air, had maybe even flowed on down the river to a place of peace. Then Mrs. Margolis started talking again, but this time her tone was incredibly different. This time, it wasn't in sorrow, but in anger that she spoke to me, and it hurt just about as much to hear it. Soon, my feeling of relief and release disappeared, only to be replaced by an unbearable tension.

"We taught her to be a giving person, Jenny, and she was, and it may be that that killed her. Not the evening of her death, nothing so direct as that. She wasn't even carrying money, because she'd spent it on coffee, so she literally had nothing to give. Although if someone had approached her for help, she would have given of herself, as she always did. No, I am talking of an earlier time. Years before, when she met Steven. He is a man who needs so much attention, and she gave it all to him. He needs an audience, and she provided that for him. He cannot support himself, and so she gave him a place to live and money to live on. We gave her a trust fund that allowed them to rent that apartment, gave it to her as a wedding present, and now he will keep their home and take that money as well. He has no shame about taking and no sense of the need to return something of equal value to the giver. He couldn't be bothered with taking her out to nice restaurants on her birthday, couldn't go to the trouble even of buying her a gift, and they spent every one of her birthdays in some bar, with Carol listening to her husband play for free."

She stopped talking. I had nearly stopped breathing.

Mr. Margolis spoke next, as the Staten Island Ferry plied past the Statue of Liberty into the port at the lower end of Manhattan. I wished I were on it. His voice was a sweet tenor, and I thought I remembered that Carol had mentioned he used to be a cantor in their synagogue. His words about Steve and Carol had a chantlike quality that made me wonder if he often repeated them to himself and to his wife.

"He has taken her life. He has taken the life of our daughter. He will take the home we made possible for them to have. He will take the money we gave her. He will take it all, her life, her money. She gave him love, but that wasn't enough for him. She gave him a home, but it wasn't enough. She gave him the sweetness and grace and joy of her existence, but he wanted the last drop of blood for himself."

His wife took up the dirge, and I half-closed my eyes against the awful, unwelcome sound of them.

"We cannot prove Steve hired some thug to kill Carol. But we know it in our hearts and our souls and in the depth of our love for our daughter. Jenny, my husband and I request that you be our eyes in that apartment and on those streets and as you go about doing Carol's good work. If you see anything, if you detect a single small thing that might unravel the dirty fabric of that man's hideous guilt, we only ask that you tell us. It is not so very much to ask, is it?"

It wasn't, not so very much.

Except that I kind of liked the man they were accusing, and Carol had, at least at one time, loved him, and I felt as if I were being asked to betray him.

"All right." I heard two echoing sighs.

"What did she tell you about him?" Mrs. Margolis asked.

"He asked me to give this to you . . ." I pulled from my briefcase the album of Carol's childhood and gave it to them. ". . . and to convey to you that he is innocent of the crime you lay on him." I heard myself mimicking their cadence but couldn't stop myself, its pull was so hypnotic.

"Tell him," Evelyn Margolis said, staring at the first page of photographs, "that you did as he asked."

"Tell him," her husband said, and he rubbed his arm as if

his bones ached, "that we hope he dies a slow death, that his blood leaks out over some cold, uncaring pavement, as Carol's did, and that he has time, as she did, to consider the fact of his approaching death. Tell him that if we can arrange it, he will never live to spend a penny of her estate."

The wind picked up off the river, and I felt chilled.

"But why?" I asked them. "Why would he kill her?"

"Steven wants to produce a record album," Mrs. Margolis said. It sounded so banal that for a moment I couldn't believe she was serious about it as a motive for murder. Then I recalled that countless people have been killed for sillier reasons, and this one might not be so trivial, not if it inspired greed and ambition. "Of course, he hasn't that much money, and that was one thing that Carol couldn't provide for him, not without getting it from us, and there was no way we could finance such a venture. For that, we wouldn't give her money. For anything else she asked, yes, but not that. But if he inherits, he could borrow on the trust fund, or he could sell off the stocks. The money Marty and I gave to our baby as her wedding gift! I will never forgive us." He put his arm around her and pulled her tightly in toward him. Some marriages, I knew, couldn't survive the death of a child, much less the murder of one. But this marriage would last at least as long as their desire for retribution; they were newly wed in their hatred of their son-in-law. She stared accusingly at her husband, and he accepted it and offered it right back to her with the implacable look in his eyes that matched the expression in hers. "We, Marty and I, we put the cheese in front of the nose of the vicious, hungry, greedy rat."

Mrs. Margolis took my hand again, and I let her hold it, although I had to repress a shudder. As I stood up, she tightened her grip and stared up at me with eyes full of the dead life of hatred. "We're counting on you, my husband and I."

"She was a friend of mine," I said.

"Remember that," Mr. Margolis warned me.

I slid my hand free, briefly bowed my head to them both, and then walked on trembling legs toward the entrance to the promenade. *Friend of mine, friend of mine, Carol, you were a friend of mine.* My loyalty, I decided, literally shaking my head to clear the spooky cobwebs from it, would be to the truth.

BUT I WOULDN'T WANT TO *DIE* THERE

And maybe that would be to find some single piece of evidence to suggest that the man Carol had once loved enough to marry had *not* killed her.

I walked faster into the spreading twilight.

9

FEELING DAZED AFTER MY INTERVIEW WITH CAROL'S PAR-
ents, I walked the quiet residential streets of Brooklyn Heights
until I found myself in a bizarre world of Arabic shops and
restaurants. *Good,* I thought, as I wandered in and out of door-
ways of an unlikely scene that seemed to arise from this upper-
class neighborhood in Brooklyn like a surrealistic mirage: *Another
world suits me fine.* I felt as if I'd been on a job interview.
*Ms. Cain, we're hiring a spy to betray our son-in-law. Your
qualifications look excellent. Would you like to apply? The
fringe benefits are interesting: fear and suspicion, and we'll
throw in guilt, if you'd like that, too.* I bought a leather ankle
bracelet with bells on it and wrapped it around my left ankle
before I left the shop. I ate tabouli with mint leaves and ratatou-
ille in a cafe with an outdoor patio in the rear, and I downed
lethal quantities of Moroccan espresso without even worrying
if it would keep me awake all night. On this night, I had a
feeling I would sleep like the dead. In a dead woman's bed. I
shook my left foot under the table to jingle the bells to call me
back to reality. The talldarkhandsome man at the next table
looked up and a corner of his full mouth twitched, as if he'd just
recalled a pleasant memory. I, too, had a sudden recollection: of
Carol, exasperated, talking about how her parents were experts
at manipulation and guilt.

"No kidding!" I muttered into my espresso.
The dark man looked over and smiled at me.

It was still twilight when I left the cafe, probably light enough to walk safely back across the bridge into Manhattan. But I was too zonked, physically and emotionally, to do it, and I didn't know how fast night fell around here. Maybe when the sun got to the other side of the skyscrapers, all light disappeared from the city. I was afraid of getting to the middle of the bridge and suddenly finding myself alone, in the dark, with whatever kind of humanity haunts bridges at night.

Going home by subway was also unthinkable. Maybe other peoples' phobias are unreasonable and illogical, but mine made perfect sense and could be easily understood by any normal person living in Tulsa, Oklahoma, or Boise, Idaho. It was only crazy New Yorkers who persisted in the illusion that their subways were desirable places to be, given other options on this earth. On this point, and this one only, I was one hundred percent with my husband, but when it came to New York, he was wrong about everything else.

As I stood in front of the cafe, attempting to hail a taxi, I mentally reviewed for Geof's benefit my first day in the city.

Hadn't everybody been kind and friendly and helpful?

All right, I had to admit there was that one cab driver who couldn't have told a one-way street from a six-lane highway. And, okay, there had been Mr. Daley Bread in 5C who was not, perhaps, the soul of congeniality. But wasn't there Mrs. Golding and her cakes? And Jed? Well, okay, there were those two guys who escaped through the restaurant windows without paying their tab, but how often did that happen? And the old man and the young van driver yelling epithets at each other, so okay. But wasn't there Steve Wolff, who was perfectly nice? Except that maybe he was a murderer, according to his former in-laws. So, all right, and maybe Pat Vinitsky was a shade abrupt, a touch brittle, but who's perfect?

Honestly—honey, I said to my husband—by and large it has been so far a perfectly normal day with average people in your typical large American city. Right, I heard his voice rebut. As normal as borrowing a dead woman's apartment and taking her job, weeping your eyes out beside a river, getting lost in cabs, all in a day's work. Nothing to it, a breeze, more than thirteen million people do it every day. But not me, my husband argued.

Back there on the promenade, Carol's mother had asked me one other thing about Steve Wolff, a question that I had managed to lose in the process of presenting the photo album to her.

"What did she tell you about him?"

"The usual," I could have replied, but I was afraid she'd make too much out of anything I said. I would only have meant: the usual bitches and gripes and *kvetches* that a wife voices to other women about her husband. He doesn't pick up his socks or he complains that she doesn't pick up hers. He never talks to her or he monopolizes every conversation. He's lousy in bed or he's insatiable and she's sick of it. He picks on her friends or he picks *up* her friends. He's stingy or he's a spendthrift. He's lazy or he's a workaholic. He's no fun or he only wants to have fun. I could have told them: "Sometimes she spoke fondly of him and sometimes she was annoyed with him. We didn't spend much time on husbands, not if everything was going all right; we talked about our work, mutual acquaintances, dreams, ambitions, philosophy, other things."

When a cab pulled over, I already had my map out, ready to show him how to get to Manhattan if he didn't happen to know.

"Riverside Drive, between Seventy-ninth and Eightieth," I directed.

"Reeversigh Drigh?"

I opened the map and pointed.

Clearly, the day wasn't over yet.

Good God, I thought in half-amusement, half-horror, what would the night bring?

It did fall suddenly over the city, leaving me in a darkened cab heading north at a nice, civilized pace on West End Avenue. South of the bus station, we passed a district of low brick buildings that ran along the eastern edge of the river. They looked like warehouses maybe. The streets in front of them looked deserted; the few lights cast dim bluish shadows on empty doorfronts and covered windows.

I noticed that the streets were not completely empty.

A young woman stood in the middle of one of them, her back to the river, her face to the passing traffic on the avenue. She looked young, with her hair all fixed up, and she was dressed up in a glittery halter top with a tight black skirt and high heels. She was just standing there, one hip cocked, staring straight ahead. That one was a white woman. Or girl, I couldn't tell which from the cab. When I turned my head to the right, I saw two black women—or girls—standing together in the middle of the opposite street. There were four young women similarly positioned in the center of the side streets for the next four blocks. They looked pretty from a distance. No other human beings were visible on their turf, although I was pretty sure there had to be men waiting in the wings, those guys who hold the knives and take the money. I'd been to Rio de Janeiro once: This operation would have seemed like a step up to those Brazilian women who came from the countryside to find a career in the big city. In Rio, you started with the live sex acts in nightclubs and moved *up* to prostitution.

"This is a great land of opportunity," I murmured.

"Oh, yes it ees," said my driver.

I thought of the novelist who'd written, "Down these mean streets a man must go." Well, sure, I thought, if he wanted to get laid. Or AIDS. But it didn't take a mean street to kill you. All it took was one mean person on a nice street. Like this street—West End Avenue. It was probably a perfectly decent street where Carol had died, only a little further north. So who was the indecent person who'd fouled it?

10

YET ANOTHER SMALL PACKAGE WRAPPED IN TINFOIL AND TIED with a bow sat in front of my—Carol's—apartment door. The door wasn't locked, but I didn't know that until the force of my key in the lock propelled me into the living room.

"Hi, Jenny."

My hand, the one holding the little gift, went to my heart, which somewhat squashed the baked goods. I stared at the male figure coming from the kitchen. He held a cup and saucer in one hand and was stirring with the spoon he held in the other.

" 'Bout time you got home."

"You scared me! What's your middle name?"

"David, why?"

"Steven David Wolff, you scared me to death."

He grinned and sat down at the little round wooden dining table. "Sorry. Didn't mean to. How's it going? You talk to them?"

"Steve, you don't live here right now."

He feigned innocence. "You mean you don't want me just walking in?"

"That's what I mean, no offense."

"Some taken." But he kept the smile on his face. "Well, hell, what do you expect me to do, Jenny? I was in the neighbor-

66

hood, and there's something I want to show you, and what was I supposed to do, go sit in the park and wait for the muggers to come out when my own apartment is sitting right here, with its key in my pocket? I didn't intend to give you cardiac arrest."

"Fine." My heart was, indeed, pounding wildly. I set down my things on the nearest chair but then pushed them off onto the floor and sat in the chair. "All right. This time. But please, next time, call first. Or knock. When I'm already in the room, okay? What is it you want to show me?"

"Change your shoes again. We have to walk there." He bent down to peer at my feet. "Keep the ankle bracelet."

I picked up the foil offering from the floor, unwrapped it, and sniffed. Pumpkin bread.

"What a sweetie," I said.

"I know, but thank you, it's always nice when people notice."

"No, I meant Mrs. Golding. Oh, forget it. I'm not walking anywhere else except to a hot bath, and you can't follow me there. I'm not even going out for dinner. I'm really beat, Steve."

"It won't take long."

"More than ten steps in any direction is too far."

He put on a woebegone face.

"Okay, okay, give me a hint."

Steve took a moment to stir the liquid in his cup, looking away from me to do it. "I want to show you where Carol died." When I didn't respond to that, he added, "Please?"

Thinking about the Margolis's accusations, I hesitated. But maybe I *should* see the spot.

"Give me a minute to slip on some jeans, Steve."

On my way into the bathroom to change clothes, I handed him the pumpkin bread. By the time I emerged, feeling luxuriously comfortable in old jeans, soft old cotton turtleneck, and my tennis shoes, he'd eaten the whole thing, and all that was left was the foil. Not to worry that I'd starve to death for lack of it, however. When we left the apartment, we nearly stepped on the two more little packages lying there.

On the first floor, we heard voices raised in the rear apartment where Jed's mother lived. As we opened the first of the two exit doors, Jed appeared in the far doorway, and a woman's furious voice carried out into the hallway with him. "You think I should forgive you anything just because you're my son! Well, listen to me, boy, there are some things that even a mother won't forgive!"

As Jed approached us, crossing the long hallway with his lanky stride, Steve covered up the awkwardness by saying quickly, "Hey, Jed, my man, how you doin' ?"

Like Steve, I pretended to have been deaf to what we'd heard.

"Where you guys off to?" Jed asked us. He didn't seem embarrassed at all and even asked in a kidding way, "Can I go, too?" With a casual jerk of his head in the direction of his mother's apartment, he said, "Anything to escape *that*. You'd think no son ever took a drink before. Jeez, I can get blotto if I want, without my *mother*"—he raised his voice to make sure she overheard him—"getting all bent out of shape over it. So, where you goin'?"

"I'm taking Jenny to see where Carol died."

Jed's eyebrows rose high in his wide forehead. "Wow."

"Private pilgrimage, Jed. Sorry."

The teenager pointed to the foil packages in our hands. "Offerings?"

Steve unwrapped his and found oatmeal cookies inside. "Carol loved Mrs. Golding's cookies. Yeah, good idea, Jed. Maybe we'll leave these there on the street for her. What do you think?"

"Leave her a cup of coffee, too, for me, man."

Steve smiled and tossed the little package to Jed. I handed mine to him, too, and Jed looked like a happy pup as he ushered us outdoors. When I looked back, he was chewing on a cookie and staring after us with a thoughtful expression on his open face.

"What do you think a mother can't forgive?" I asked Steve.

We turned east on Eighty-sixth Street, trotting along at a typical New York City clip, which was about twice as fast as we walked back home. Attempting to maintain at least some dignity, I tried not to pant as I spoke.

He shrugged, looking at the traffic. "He probably didn't clean his room."

"You don't think it's what he said?"

"That he was drunk? Probably. I do know he doesn't do illicit substances, because I kept offering him some, and he kept turning me down, until finally he told me straight out that he'd rather drink."

"What does he do, Steve, besides man the door for his mother?"

"Boy the door, you mean? I don't know that Jed can *man* anything."

"Well, that's a little cruel, don't you think?"

"Well, you're a little judgmental, don't you think?"

We walked in silence for a moment.

"Don't say it," he said. "Don't say, 'That's okay, Steve, I know this is hard on you.' "

"I was going to say, 'Don't be a jerk, Steve.' "

He laughed in a burst of noise that sounded as if he were releasing tension. "Okay, he has some other part-time job."

"What kind of illicit substances do *you* do?"

"What kind do you want?"

"You'll give musicians a bad name."

He laughed even louder at that, which surprised me.

It wasn't *that* funny.

"I'm taking you the general route she ran," he explained, looking tenser and grimmer by the moment. I kept still, letting him do the talking and the leading. "I guess it wasn't always the same way. Sometimes she'd run the park, but not at night. For night runs, she was on the streets. She ran over to Central Park West, started threading her way back this way, following the green lights, probably, stopped on Amsterdam for coffee, and ended up where I'm going to take you on West End Avenue. *Ended*. *End*. Yeah, she did that, all right."

On Amsterdam, he steered me into a twenty-four-hour restaurant called Cafe O'Lay.

"Is this Irish or a hangout for whores?" I couldn't help but ask.

"Irish/Spanish. Try the *latte*, it'll pump you up for the night."

"Great, just what I need when all I want to do is sleep."

"Get decaf then."

We each purchased almond *biscottis* and cafe *lattes* to go. The cookies were a good seven inches long for dipping, and the coffee was served in tall cardboard cups that were so hot to the touch we had to wrap them in napkins. From big silver shakers on the counter we shook out powdered cinnamon, nutmeg, and chocolate onto the frothy, milky coffee.

"Hi, Mr. Wolff," said the white-aproned older man behind the counter. "You're getting to be a regular like your wife was. That's nice." But he looked at me suspiciously, as if to say, But what are you doing out with another woman so soon?

"Thanks, Mr. Malloy," Steve said. "This is a friend of Carol's. I was telling Jenny here how Carol always stopped here for coffee when she ran, even that last time."

"She was here not ten minutes before that goddamned animal killed her," the old man told me, fury empurpling his face and shaking his voice. Tears came to his eyes. "If I'd kept her talking for five minutes more—"

"Come on, Mr. Malloy," Steve said. "Stop that, you know—"

"Well, it's true! Five minutes! That's all! I couldn't ask about the weather? I had to be in such a hurry to serve her, I couldn't take the time to ask how is she doing, how's the work, what does she think the Mets are going to do this season?"

"She was probably in a hurry herself," Steve consoled him.

"Oh, she'd have humored an old man, she'd have stopped to talk to me if I'd bothered to show any simple courtesy, that's the kind of woman your wife was. Always a nice smile, always a kind word. If only I'd made her stay so I could hear more of those nice words from her that night! Hell, I could have complained about how I didn't have enough help, how my dishwasher didn't come in, I could have said *some*thing." Mr. Malloy rubbed down his counter with a wet rag. "Something. I think about it every day now, especially every evening when I come in and she don't. No, don't you offer me any money, Mr. Wolff, you'll insult me if you do."

"I can't keep coming in here and getting free coffee off you. It isn't right, Mr. Malloy."

"It *is* right," the old man declared. "It makes me feel better. And don't you think you'll save me any money if you stop

coming in. Then I'll just give away a cup every morning in your
honor. Or hers. Hell, I'll give it to the first bum shows his face
on the street, attract a whole school of them bums, and they'll
be a hell of a nuisance, and it'll be your fault, 'cause you
wouldn't come in, 'cause you wouldn't let a old man make up
for not keeping your poor wife for five more minutes of
conversation."

"Okay, okay!" Steve showed his palms in capitulation.

"Thank you," I chimed in.

But the old man suddenly looked up at me. "Not you. You,
I don't know. You, I got no reason to feel bad about. Him, he
goes free. You still pay."

I was startled but laughing as I handed over my money.

He pointed to a cardboard coffee cup that sat on his counter.
"Don't forget the tip."

I contributed a quarter from my change, glancing at Steve.

"You're a trip, Mr. Malloy," he said. "Carol liked you."

"You don't know that," the old man said.

"I guess you're right. I don't know that. Okay, then, I like
you."

Malloy looked over at me. "What about you? Do you like
me?"

"Not particularly," I said.

We all grinned at each other. Then, dipping our *biscottis* and
slurping our coffee, Steve and I stepped back outside.

"Is he what you'd call a New York character?" I inquired.

Steve gave me a look of surprise. "You think he's odd?"

I rolled my eyes. "Never mind. Show me."

We walked south and stopped two blocks later in front of an
all-night laundromat. "There." Steve pointed in the direction
of an orange metal trash receptacle shaped like a basketball
hoop. "That's where she died. You go look. That's where her
body was. I can't go any closer. I'm scared to death I'll see
stains or something."

I walked, barely breathing, toward the trash can.

11

❧

B<small>UT THERE WASN'T ANYTHING GRUESOME TO VIEW, ONLY AN</small> ordinary sidewalk with ordinary wear and tear. No blood stains that I could detect, nothing upsetting to see, only something distressing to visualize and to feel in my gut and my heart.

"I wash it every day for week."

I turned to find that a middle-aged woman had come up beside me. She looked of Oriental descent and had some kind of accent. Not Indian. Not Japanese. I wasn't sure which. Thai, like our waitress at lunch? No, maybe Vietnamese. We didn't often have these dilemmas of ethnic identification back home in Port Frederick.

"Trying to get blood out," she said. "Make people feel bad. Scare children." Then she waved at Steve, who hadn't come a single step closer. "Poor fellow. He come every day, too. Lonesome. You marry now?"

"Yes, I'm married."

"No, I mean, you marry him now?"

"No, I'm just a friend. And I'm already married. I mean . . ." I gave it up. "No."

"How you doin', Mr. Wolff?" she called to him. "He ask, Do I see anything, but I say no, my son, he was here that night, and customers, but they old and drunk, they no see anything.

72

They hear, though, and my son, he go running out, he see somebody run away. A man, he say. Jog suit, hood over head, no tell whether black or white or what color man. But big, like a man, my son say. He say he thinks he saw before, saw the man before, but who can tell from back? I tell cops this, I tell Mr. Wolff all this. But he keep come back, like he maybe find her again, like she maybe one day run by here, say hello, like she do. Very friendly woman, Mrs. Wolff."

"Margolis," I said automatically. "Carol Margolis."

"That you name? My name Orchid Lei. My son married, too, but not happy. You not happy with your husband, you come back, do laundry, no charge, meet my son. He tell you all about it."

"Thank you," I said, backing away as tactfully but as rapidly as I could. "Nice to meet you."

"Bye, Mr. Wolff!" she called.

I saw him give her a half wave in response.

"Is *she* what you'd call a New York character?" I inquired.

"She's what you call a ghoul." He grabbed my elbow to steer me off the curb and a couple of feet into the street where vehicles were whizzing by in the dark on West End. "She took one of the rags she used to clean up the sidewalk and she pinned it up on the wall of her laundromat with a notice about which cleaning detergents work the best on difficult stains. I hate her."

"My God. Do you want me to go back and tear it down?"

"I asked her son to, but he said I shouldn't take it personal."

"Nice people. She said her son saw the murderer."

"It's a publicity gimmick."

I stared at him. "What?"

"Watch it, Jenny! That taxi almost gave you a free ride. Yeah, a gimmick to get more business into the laundromat. He let the word out on the street that he saw something, and people dropped by to hear the story, which got better and more detailed as the days went by. The murderer started out about five foot six, according to his first story, but he grew to about six foot five with a huge scar under his left eye, and he was missing an ear, and he was black, and he had an earring in the remaining ear, and he threatened Mrs. Lei's son with disembowelment if he breathed a word of any of this to anybody."

"Mrs. Lei's son must be very brave then," I said dryly, "to divulge so much."

"I think Mrs. Lei's son likes to run the laundromat so he can sniff dirty underwear."

"Who else saw something, really saw something?"

"Nobody who'll say anything, if anybody did. I've asked, all up and down the street, and I keep coming back and asking different people or figuring out who are the ones who are almost always around at that time of night and talking to them, but nobody knows nuthin' 'bout nuthin' 'round here. And the funny thing is, I believe them, Jenny. It was getting dark, there was a lot of traffic, a lot of noise, a lot going on, and if you were trying to rob somebody it was a fairly good time and a good place."

"On a city street? With cars going by?"

"Yeah, but they're watching traffic. Some guy's in a jogging suit, he runs up right next to a woman who's also in a running suit, he stops her, they talk, he moves closer and sticks a knife in her, she falls, he bends down and pretends to ask if she's all right, then he runs off like he's going for help. Who's going to stop?"

"That's what happened?"

"My best guess."

We had reached the other side of the street, and now I briefly touched his hand that held his coffee cup. "How long are you going to keep coming over here like this, Steve? How long are you going to keep asking questions?"

"Have you talked to my in-laws yet?"

I'd been hoping he wouldn't ask again. "This afternoon."

"You give them the album, my message?"

"You don't want to know what they said."

"Well, then that's how long I'll keep coming over here, Jenny. That's how long I'll keep asking questions of perfect strangers. Until I get a different response out of Evelyn and Marty Margolis. Until I hear them say, We're sorry, we were wrong, you're innocent, we apologize, we get on our fucking *knees*—"

"Steve," I said and touched his wrist again.

He lowered his voice. "That's how long."

"I'm really tired," I told him.

"Me, too. Let's go home. You go to my home. I'll go sleep on the couch at my friends' place. What kind of crazy world is this anyway? Listen, keep your eyes open for me, will you? Maybe you'll hear something or see something to help me find the killer."

I didn't tell him the Margolises had requested the same thing, only the killer they wanted me to nail was Steve. "It doesn't seem likely I will. A street killing. By a stranger. What am I going to hear or see?"

He shrugged off my objections. "It may be a big city, but it's a small town in many ways. People know things, there are connections, people are tied together in incredible ways that never fail to knock me out. You never know, is what I'm saying, so . . . you never know." I thought he looked tired enough to sleep in a doorway.

"Is it safe for me to walk back by myself?"

"Sure, but come out later. I've got a gig. Come hear me."

"Oh, Steve, I'm sorry, but I have to work tomorrow."

He smiled unhappily. "That sounds familiar."

"Maybe when Geof gets here this weekend. Where are you playing?"

He named a place, Lucille's, and an address that was meaningless to me, on Tenth Avenue.

"I don't even know what kind of musician you are, Steve."

"A good one." He laughed. "Keyboard. Blues, jazz, contemporary stuff. Bring the hubby. I'll ask him about the case."

I tossed my empty cup in a trash bin, another orange basketball hoop like the one beside which Carol died, and I gave his shoulders a quick squeeze. He tossed his own cup away and pulled me in for a real hug. I tried not to think about the fact that I had just hugged a man whose in-laws thought had murdered my friend Carol. With a jaunty wave that made me feel sad, he walked off into the brightly lit New York City night, leaving me on my own.

12

I TROTTED BACK HOME, FEELING SCARED ALL THE WAY.

The scrawny little trees on the sidewalks seemed larger at night, with trunks that looked big enough for muggers to hide behind. The below-pavement stoops and stairwells looked like deep pools of black water in which octopuses in human form might be swimming, just waiting to snake out their tentacles to snare my ankles. Picking up my speed, I ran from one pool of streetlamp illumination to another, turning onto Riverside Drive with relief, until I noticed how dark the park was across the street. I raced to the front doors of the brownstone. There were no lights turned on outside or even on the first floor to help me maneuver the key in the locks, so I had to do it all in relative darkness, convinced the whole time that Carol's killer was going to pounce on my back at any moment. Flinging myself into the foyer and locking the two doors behind me soothed my terror but only momentarily.

"Damn!" I said, fumbling along the wall. "Where's a light?"

Jed hadn't told me they turned off the hall lights at night, and he hadn't shown me where the switch was. I groped around with my hands to the right of the doors and then to the left. Nothing. There wasn't any light glimmering around the edges of Jed's door, but there was around the rim of his mother's. As

my eyes adjusted to the dark—and I got over my panic a little—
that diluted glow helped me to locate the stairs.

I stared up toward the first landing.

Pitch black up there.

"Great," I muttered. "Calm down, it's just a house."

My right hand found the railing, but that felt insecure to me,
so I slid my feet over to the wall and commenced to hug that
on my way upstairs. Around my ankle, the bells of the Arabic
bracelet jingled, announcing my small progress in the dark. The
sound made me nervous, so I stooped, fumbled, took the
damned silly thing off, and stuck it in my pocket. As I slowly
climbed in the dark, I recited to myself: "The doors were firmly
locked when you came in." Second step, third, fourth. "The
only part of this reality that you don't like is the darkness,
obviously, but what if you were blind?" Fifth, sixth, seventh.
"And, anyway, the darkness wouldn't exist if you knew how to
turn on the lights." Where was the darned first landing, hadn't
I climbed a good twenty steps? "Pretend it's light in here,
pretend you can see just fine. And remember you can scream
if anything goes wrong. What's to go wrong?" My left foot raised
itself for the next step, but came down in thin air. "Shit. Found
the landing. Don't fall. Okay, follow the wall around to the next
set of stairs. Don't think about the stairwell, and especially
don't think about it when you get to the fifth floor, where it's
five stories down to the bottom. Don't think about that.

"What's this? Door frame. Door."

My hand and body did as instructed, passing one closed door,
then another. Shit, I didn't like this, didn't like this feeling that
I might come across a door that wasn't closed, but rather one
that was wide open, with somebody waiting inside of a room,
and me, losing my balance in the gaping hole of an open door,
stumbling, falling into the waiting, malevolent darkness.

"Door number three. Closed. Now, stairs up. Why the *hell*
can't they leave the hall lights on at night? How much money
do they think they're going to save in electricity, for heaven's
sake? Not as much as they'll lose on their insurance when I
make a wrong turn and grab for the railing and miss and fly
downstairs to break my neck and sue them, that's for sure.
"Up, step, up, step, up step, shit, step, shit, step. What's that
noise?"

Brahms's *Requiem?* Coming from Mrs. Amory's apartment, 2C? Great, just what a person wants to hear when she's scared to death, a requiem! The dramatic music beckoned me onto that floor and then followed me higher.

I had two more floors to go, and things were not getting any brighter the closer I got to the moon. Didn't anybody stay up past nine o'clock in this joint? Wasn't anybody home besides poor, crazy Mrs. Amory?

Finally, about the time I reached the next landing, I'd had it.

"Hello!" I called out loud. "Hello! Is anybody here? Excuse me! How do you turn on the hall lights?"

The music stopped.

I heard footsteps far above me, and then I heard a door open and suddenly there was a thrill of illumination down the stair shaft.

"Who is it?" called down a scared-sounding female voice.

I called back up. "Mrs. Golding? It's me, Carol's friend. Would you keep the light on? I'll be right up!"

Suddenly, lights came on up and down the stairwell.

I scurried on up to five, where Ida Golding stood waiting for me, smiling tentatively and clutching her assortment of cardigan sweaters to her chest. Her white hair stood out all over her head, so that she looked like Einstein's sister.

"I'm sorry," I said, panting by the time I reached her. "I hope I didn't scare you. I couldn't find any light switches, and I was afraid I'd trip and kill myself on the way up."

"That man!" she said mysteriously.

"Jed?"

She shook her head, her lips pursed tightly together in a severe display of disapproval. "Him!" She pointed a gnarled finger at the door of 5C, where my other neighbor, Daley Bread, lived. "I know he turns them off every chance he gets, when nobody's looking. He says we're spendthrifts to leave them on when nobody's out there. As if we don't want them on for security! As if there might not be some poor soul like you, who doesn't know how to turn them on from the front hall. Honestly, it would serve him right if you'd fallen and broken your neck!" It didn't seem to occur to her that might hurt me a bit more than it would hurt him.

"Where are the switches, Mrs. Golding?"

She pointed to a vertical button arrangement placed high outside my own door. I'd seen them before without realizing what they were. "There's one on each floor. The awful thing, though, is that if"—she jerked her head toward 5C—"*he* sneaks out and turns them off, you have to use a flashlight to find the button to turn them on again, and Mrs. Goodman won't do anything about it!"

"Mrs. Goodman?" I asked.

I was then interrupted by a querulous voice coming from inside of 5C.

"Ida! You stop that lying now! I mean it! I'll tell!"

"Oh, you shut up!" she surprised me by yelling back.

"I'll tell everything! I will, Ida!"

She looked frightened at that, and she leaned toward me and whispered, "He's a crazy old man!" In a more normal tone of voice, she said, "Mrs. Goodman, you know, Jed's mother."

Ah, my landlady. I chose not to announce right there in the hallway that I planned to have a little talk with Mrs. Goodman. If she didn't know how to coerce better behavior from her owners, I did from long experience dealing with foundation clients who didn't always live up to contractual expectations. I'd be damned if I was going to let a cranky, stingy old man endanger my life or that of anybody else in this building. I was of half a mind to pound on his door and confront him about it right then.

"Did you get my surprises, dear?"

I stifled my anger at him and smiled down at her. "Oh, yes, they're wonderful. Thanks so much, Mrs. Golding. Was it you, by any chance, who put a basket of food for me in my refrigerator?"

She smiled and blushed, looking so cute and nice and lovable that I bent to give her cheek an impulsive kiss of thanks, even though I did wish people would stop letting themselves into my living quarters whenever they pleased. She grabbed my left wrist in an affectionate grasp, but then her grip tightened and began to hurt my flesh. I peeled away from her and saw that the expression on Mrs. Golding's face had altered, no, frozen, into a sugary parody of her usual sweet smile, and it seemed to be directed not at me, but at somebody over my shoulder.

I turned and looked, but all I saw was Daley Bread's closed door. Maybe I had only imagined it, I thought, because when I looked at her again, the sweetness had reappeared in her eyes and she'd released her death's grip on my wrist. The spooky moment passed as if it had never been.

"Well, goodnight," I said rather quickly.

"Sweet dreams, Carol," she said.

"Jenny," I reminded her. "It's Jenny."

But she only smiled over her shoulder as she slipped back into her apartment. Oh, lord, I thought, as I heard her bolts click, what kind of sweet old dingbat do we have here? I glanced at 5C. And there? I resolved to carry a flashlight with me when I went out at night. When I put the key in my own lock and then brought up my left hand to open the door, I saw an angry red band around it, as if I'd snapped a bracelet too tight.

I wanted to talk to a cop, preferably the one I was married to, but I was tired and city-gritty, and I knew it would feel good to be bathed and fresh when I called him. Considering Geof's low opinion of this city, I wanted to sound calmer and cooler by the time he heard my voice. I'd panicked over nothing. He perceived enough real threats in New York without adding my fantasies to them.

To calm myself, I slowly opened up the sofa-bed, stacking the cushions on the floor and then pulling out the mattress. It was already neatly fitted with flowered sheets and a thin yellow blanket. The pillows I located on a shelf in the clothes closet; they were thick, soft mounds of feathers covered with cotton cases of the quality that seem to stroke the lucky face that lies on them, as if to say, "There, there, everything's going to be all right now." I used the rheostat to turn the overhead lights down low and then I finished unpacking and I arranged my toiletries where I wanted them to go in the big white porcelain bathroom. Steve had been right: Carol's parents seemed to have left all her belongings, so that I had to scoot her underwear over to fit mine in and scooch over her clothes on their hangers to make room for mine. I recognized certain suits and dresses, but it was her underwear that finally made me smile over the lump that had resurfaced in my throat.

"You, too?" she'd said the first time we roomed together at a convention. "I can't believe it!"

We had both just peeled off our conservative gray business suits, and there we stood, revealed to one another in similar red silk lingerie. It was easy to remember the burst of hilarity that followed on the heels of our mutual discovery that we were both secret lingerie collectors. Bikini panties, lacy teddies, push-up bras, those were the slippery, sensual secrets that lay between wool and skin during business meetings. Nobody knew except us and our husbands. And now, each other. So it became a standing joke, an annual exchange of holiday gifts, each more outrageously provocative than the last, and expensive shopping trips when we'd sneak off during conventions to prowl the finest lingerie departments. It was difficult to know who enjoyed our silly, secret vice more, us or our fortunate husbands. It got so that when I told Geof I was off to a meeting out of town where I'd see Carol, he'd grin lasciviously, lick his lips, and say, "Great! I can't wait to see what you're wearing when you get back!"

I closed the drawer on our underwear.

The simple domestic tasks of getting settled had slowed my heartbeat and steadied my breathing, so that by the time I slipped into a big hot tubful of bubbly water, I was nearly relaxed.

"Ahh," I sighed as I leaned back.

It was heaven, Carol's big porcelain tub with the claw feet. Big enough for two, I decided, even for a long-legged mare like me and my big, beefy husband. Geof had been doing more desk work in the last couple of years since he'd made lieutenant, and the sedentary life was starting to show up around his shoulders, his chest, and especially his midriff. He'd taken up running and gone back to lifting weights, but it was proving hard for him to whittle his waist back down to where he liked it. I didn't care, as long as he felt good and remained healthy, I didn't mind the love handles or the cushiony feel of the crook between his shoulder and his chest, where I rested my head before we went to sleep. I liked walking my hand down the hair on his chest to his stomach and feeling the flesh give a little to my touch; anyway, he still tightened to a rock when he wanted to. But *he* wanted to get in better shape, which might mean getting out from behind his desk. But was moving him to New York City any way to do that?

I splashed water on myself to stay warm in the cooling tub. "Better not jump ahead," I warned myself. "Who said anything about moving to New York?" I'd promised him before I left that a couple of weekends of hard walking in New York would firm him up. To which he had retorted, "Yeah, there's nothing like running away from thugs to keep you in shape. You watch your step down there, Jennifer. If you get yourself killed like Carol did, I'm going to be pissed."

Such a romantic, my cop.

I called him as soon as I had tucked myself into Carol's bed. "Still alive?" he greeted me.

"Yes, I only got robbed once, raped twice, and otherwise assaulted a half-dozen times. Hello, sweetheart. You know, for a cop, you are remarkably paranoid."

"As cop, I know there is no such thing as paranoia."

I laughed. "It's all true, huh?"

"Everything you suspect, every worst thing you imagine, every nightmare you ever had, it's all true. Especially there, where you are, the city I will not name. It all comes true. Evil personified. The devil incarnates every day in . . . that city. You can see him or her—"

"Sure, if god can be a woman, so can the devil. Equal opportunity religion."

"—on every street. All those grim faces. I remember driving past a bunch of them standing on a street and they looked like the corners of buildings. Like the sharp, jutting corners of buildings, that's how their faces looked. Those are people I don't want to know. They'd stand out in a crowd up here, because you can see the badness in them. That hardness and toughness and bad-ass badness. I'd arrest every damn one of them, I'd turn into an Old West sheriff and tell them to get the hell out of my town before sunset. I'd jail them on suspicion."

Geez, he was on a riff. "Of what?"

"Of possession."

"I'll bite. Possession of what?"

"Of evil. God, I hate that place. Come home, before it gets you."

"Before I turn into a corner of a building? Yeah, that's me, all right, hard and sharp and cutting. I'll probably start beating up old ladies after I've been here a few days. We've got few in this building I could start on. You want to tell me about your day, Geof? You want to ask about mine? Or do you just want to spoil it for me?"

"This trip of yours makes me cranky."

"No kidding."

"I'm terrified that you'll want to stay there, and I'll have to move there if I want to stay married to you, which I suppose I do—"

"Well, hey, if you've got doubts—"

"And I don't fucking want to live there."

"Remember the first time we came to New York together? Remember lunch at the Plaza? Our carriage ride in the park?"

"So?"

"It was delicious, right? It was sexy and exciting and I didn't hear you bitching about New York City then. The city faded into the background, it was just this glamorous backdrop for us, and it can be that way this weekend, Geof. And let me tell you something, if you ruin it, if you bitch and moan and carry on about how much you hate it, I swear I will take this job to spite you."

"You wouldn't do that."

"No, you're right. I wouldn't do that. But *please*."

"Come on, Jenny, do you think it's really about the city? I'm talking incipient loss here, I'm talking the grief I will feel if you make this decision regardless of my feelings, regardless of our marriage, that's what this is about, not about that damned city. I'm dealing in truths about our future, and you're worried about whether or not I ruin the weekend. Can we get to another level here, Jenny, maybe a shade deeper than whether or not we're going to have *fun* from Friday through Sunday?"

"I beg your pardon! The idea that I will not consider you when I make a job decision is incredibly insulting to me. Come on, Geof! All I'm saying is, let's get through this weekend and try to enjoy it. We'll make the important decisions *together* as we always do."

"As you sometimes don't."

"Well, I don't have as much practice as you do."

I was his third wife, the other two having divorced him.

"Oooh, when she mentions the other wives, she's ticked."

"You are being really obnoxious."

He was quiet for a moment. "I'll behave."

"One way or another."

"That's true." He laughed, and his tone of voice shifted into a more familiar easiness and warmth. "Hey, did I tell you, I ran two miles tonight and got by with a salad for dinner?"

"That's why you're cranky—you're hungry."

And so we settled, finally, into "married" talk—what he did that day, what I did, who he talked to, who I did, until finally one of us was the first to say:

"I love you."

And then, "Sweet dreams."

After I hung up, feeling all glowy, I opened the drawer of the little table beside the sofa bed, hoping to find pad and paper there to write a schedule for the next day's work.

Instead, I found a gun.

It was like opening a drawer and having a cockroach scurry out of the silverware. I thought I'd escaped guns by leaving my cop at home, but here was what looked to me like a .22, an old cowboy type of pistol with a pin you pulled in front of the cylinder to release the whole assembly. I did that and found it to be fully loaded, ready to shoot. There were several other little bullets scattered loose in the drawer, like paper clips. As a cop's spouse, nothing made me madder than people casually leaving guns lying about so that bad guys could steal them and use them against my husband. When I heard of a cop being shot with a stolen gun, I wanted to kill two people: the shooter and the citizen who made the gun available for stealing.

"Is this what it takes to live in the big city?"

In Port Frederick, a woman living alone didn't need a gun, and lots of people didn't lock their doors, and I couldn't recall if anybody had *ever* been killed in a street robbery.

So much for sweet dreams.

13

I AWOKE FEELING CALM, EVEN RESTED, AS IF I'D BROKEN A
fever in my sleep. I should relax, I told myself. The police were
taking care of Carol's murder case. I was making too much out
of her message, because I felt guilty for not returning her call,
because I couldn't believe she could die like that, because I
wanted some satisfaction.

"Well, you're not going to get it," I told myself.

She was dead, that was all, so I should forget it.

I swung my legs over the side of the bed and discovered that
I was actually halfway eager to begin my first official full day
of work for Carol and the Hart Foundation.

Upon pulling the living room curtains back, I saw that I
wasn't the only person who was up so early on this beautiful
New York morning: Five stories below, a woman was seated at
a table on a small brick patio. Mrs. Goodman, the mother who'd
decreed some things unforgivable, even in a son? I could see
only the top of her head, which was blondish, and her shoulders
and back, which were covered in what looked like an orange
chenille bathrobe. She didn't look up, and I didn't call down,
"Yo! Ma!"

Cautiously, I raised the big window higher.

The vertigo wasn't so bad this time, as it had been when Jed

had raised it for me, but I still didn't have the nerve to raise
it to chest level. Waist level would do fine, I decided, so that
I wouldn't feel as if I could accidentally stumble and tumble
through. Was that the fear? Or was I afraid of being sucked
through by some invisible, consuming force of nature? Maybe
I secretly feared that I'd jump out the window, satisfying some
unconscious impulse to suicide.

"Well, hell, this is absurd," I muttered.

On purpose, to test and raise my fear threshold, I pushed
the window higher and higher, until I had it above my shoulders and even had to arch myself a little into the opening in
order to hoist the weight.

Very carefully, I pushed myself back into the room.

I was breathing harder than the exertion required.

Maybe it was all that talk about windows with Carol's parents,
Evelyn and Martin, the day before, but I suddenly had an inner
vision of a membrane, molecule thin, covering the space where
the window was open. I saw it as a membrane separating life
from sudden death. I could almost literally see it—it was flesh
color, just like skin—and it was smooth and tight, though not
so tight as a drum skin. I felt as if I could easily poke a finger
through it, opening it, bursting it like a hymen.

A person could so easily plunge through these open windows.

And to think: There were these uncovered apertures all over
this city, most of them many, many floors higher than this one,
and all of them subtly offering the choice: life or death?

I stepped closer to the window again and put out my right
hand to the open space, touched my palm to the air in it, closed
my eyes, imagined a membrane there, felt it vibrating to my
touch, sensed the ever-so-slight suction of its movement in the
light breeze. I imagined it breathing in and out: I gave it living
qualities: Could it take a sudden deep breath, like a lung, and
suck me into it, through it, so that I fell to the patio below?
That would be a hell of a way to greet my landlady. Splat. On
my back, gazing up at her with my very surprised eyes: *Why,
hello there!*

I withdrew my hand and opened my eyes.

The woman on the patio was staring up at me.

Embarrassed, I gave a little wave and stepped back out of
view.

"You are certifiable," I told myself.

But that didn't stop me from obsessing on what I began to think of as "the death membrane" as I fixed my morning coffee and warmed up one of the croissants in the wicker basket. The idea of an hymanic membrane made me think of older people I had known who, as they lay dying, seemed to slide back and forth between another realm and this one, having intercourse with death, as it were. For a little while, they'd be present in the hospital or bedroom with their living family, and then they'd be gone, eyes closed, unreachable, and when they returned from that state, they'd murmur something blissful about having "seen Daddy and Grandma" and about having heard gorgeous music and about having witnessed indescribably beautiful things. They had been sliding in and out through the death membrane . . .

I poured my coffee into a china cup and looked back over my shoulder at the wide-open window.

"It's so much more visible here," I murmured.

Death, I meant.

On my way to work—in Carol's closet office—I even whistled "New York, New York." I felt close to her as I settled down into her chair in front of her computer and I got a progressively warmer, closer feeling as I methodically went through her files for the next couple of hours. She'd been good at her job, that was easy to see. She had been efficient. She had been conscientious. She had been exactly as I would have expected her to be; it was a pleasure to "see" her at work, through her files.

So why was everybody so mad at her?

The files didn't help much when it came to trying to uncover the causes of the various emergencies I was supposed to resolve.

The file on Mrs. Marguerite Stewart included a painfully honest notation from Carol that the potential donor had backed out "because I have 'deeply offended' her." But then I wondered whether those words were meant to be sarcastic, because they were followed by the words, "The truth offendeth?" That sounded like Carol being sardonic. What truth had Carol offered to Mrs. Stewart that had "offended" the philanthropist? Whatever it was, surely the old woman couldn't have gotten herself up in a mugger disguise to stab Carol on the street! But this particular old woman had a houseful of ex-convicts on her premises . . .

Carol was frank in detailing why Dr. and Mrs. Malcolm Lloyd wanted to cut off their funding to the foundation, including a report of the episode when the doctor threw a notebook at her. I could tell that Carol had dearly loved the South Bronx neighborhood gardening project that the Hart Foundation trustees had voted to fund instead of the controversial Black Company. It sounded as if the Lloyds favored that charity because Dr. Lloyd had a relative who was involved in it. It also sounded as if the good doctor had a hell of a temper and even a violent streak.

In the file on the Upstage Theater, Carol had kept a log of the telephone calls the manager/director, Damon Calendar, had made to her to demand the payment of the next installment of their grant. "I told him I'd pay him when I saw a *dress* rehearsal," Carol had written, "and not before then." She must not have trusted them to get their show mounted. Was she afraid they'd take the money and run? I knew that foundation clients wanted to kill us if we were late with their money, but I'd never viewed that desire as anything but metaphorical, at least not until now . . .

I gathered from reading her file on Patty Vinitsky's pet project, Book'Em, that Carol had not been convinced that the project or the man behind it was on the level. She didn't come right out and write, "scam?" but I could sense her suspicions as if they were red flags littering the file. There definitely might be something illegal going on there.

I put the files away. Time for phone calls. Appointments to make, people to see, sites to evaluate, reports to write. Hot damn! I was back at work again, picking up where Carol had left off and (I had to admit) loving it, the do-good, active, familiar feel of it all.

"May I speak to Mrs. Marguerite Stewart? Yes, I'll speak to her son, instead . . ."

"Andrei Bolen? . . . I'll drop by the school this afternoon . . ."

"Yes, Mrs. Lloyd, this evening would be perfect to meet with you and your husband. You're on Central Park South, aren't you? Which building . . ."

"Is this the Upstage Theater? May I speak to Damon Calendar? I'm calling for the Hart Foundation . . ."

I dressed for work in my black suit, but this time with a pretty pale yellow silk blouse and low-heeled black shoes. (I asked Carol's advice on my selection of underwear, and my glance landed on a silky yellow set. Just right.) When I stepped outside the apartment, briefcase in hand, I found a fresh foil offering on the hall carpet.

"Damn," I muttered ungratefully, "I don't have time for this."

I was due at Mrs. Marguerite Stewart's home in Brooklyn in an hour to see if I could persuade her to change her mind again and contribute her nice well-intentioned fortune to the foundation in order to benefit the ex-convicts of New York City, a deserving population if there ever was one, although deserving of *what* was perhaps a bit of a philosophical conundrum. Oh, I was rolling, I could feel the irony kicking in, always a sure sign that I was running in high gear.

It slowed me down to have to toss the latest baked goods into the refrigerator, so I didn't. I laid them in front of Jed's door on my way out, hoping that Mrs. Golding wouldn't come downstairs and see it. Or, maybe I wanted her to. Maybe the truth was that her little surprises were beginning to feel a shade pathological to me, a bit like flowers left at graveside, especially as she seemed to confuse live me with dead Carol.

Glad to be leaving, I burst out the front doors into sunshine.

14

I'D NEVER BEEN TO BROOKLYN BEFORE YESTERDAY, AND here I was back again. But this morning, I traveled past the dignified, prosperous residential area near the promenade, where the Margolises lived with their grief and rage, and I penetrated on deeper into the territory, down Flatbush Avenue and into a strikingly different world.

Here, there were more faces of color, more varieties of human form and comeliness than I'd seen the day before. Poorer here. Rundown at the heels. Shabby, but intriguing. Lots of small shops, the kind that used to be called boutiques. Cafes. Litter. Great old houses, cheek by jowl, like so much of New York City was, and Port Frederick wasn't.

"Here you go," said the cabbie, a woman this time, as she pulled up to a corner house, a mansion, really, and one whose appearance raised the cabbie's eyebrows as well as mine. "Hey, lucky you, I've always loved this house. Spooky, like. Those turrets, that red sandstone, those peaked roofs. Big sucker. Is it still single-family?"

"Halfway house for ex-convicts, I believe."

"Well, heck, what am I doing driving a hack? I think I'll go rob a bank."

I examined the exterior of the huge old house as I walked

up the same kind of octagonal paving stones there'd been on the promenade. The place looked in excellent shape to me. If it took a lot of money to keep this monster healthy, it seemed that somebody had that money and was willing to spend it, and they had good help. The grass in the lawn was lush and barbered, even so early in the season, the black paint was shiny, the porch was swept, and even the cushions on the old black wrought-iron porch furniture appeared to have been dusted and dirt-whacked recently, so you could sit down on them without walking away with the seat of your skirt filthy. So preoccupied was I in staring at the mansion that I was startled when a man walked out the front door.

"Help you?"

He was shorter than my five-eight by a couple of inches, with an expressionless face—what they call in the psychology biz "no affect"—that was shaven smooth, as was the rest of his skull. He had very small ears, and one of them sported a small diamond. I noted his blue jeans and his denim work shirt and wondered if he was the handyman who kept this place so well maintained. He had dark, dark eyes, white skin tanned to a caramel color, and bushy gray eyebrows that looked odd on his youthfully smooth complexion.

"I'm here to see Mrs. Stewart."

"I'll tell her. Wait here."

"All right," I said, as if agreeing to something in which I'd been given a choice. Bossy little fascist. When he disappeared into the house, a streak of rebelliousness hit me, and I quietly opened the screen door and followed him into a foyer, cool and dark, with stairs that he was climbing to a second floor. He heard me and looked back. I met his eyes, unsmiling, and didn't blink until he turned away to complete his climb. Tell *me* to "wait here," Charlie!

While he was gone, I looked around. I saw a large dining room with a table to which ten chairs were pulled up and ten places neatly set. That was to my left; to my right was a living room with elegant appointments, dusted, vacuumed, completely tidy. Upstairs, I glimpsed a landing with a large chest that looked like a bride's wish chest and great leaded windows that would have let in a lot of light if a huge old oak tree weren't blocking the sun.

He reappeared at the top of the stairs.

"She says, Come up."

"Thank you," I said carefully and politely and commenced to climb under his dark-eyed stare. If it hadn't been for the gray eyebrows, I'd have pegged him to be in his thirties, but he might be as much as twenty years older than that. As I got closer to him, he didn't make any move to slide out of my way, so that for a moment it looked as if I might have to walk over him. No way was *I* going to walk around! And then I suddenly thought: Whoa! What am I doing? Strange house, strange—very strange—man. How do I know there's really a Mrs. Stewart somewhere up there? What am I doing, just docilely ascending to within reach of this man with the tanned, muscular forearms and the physique of a small bull?

In that space of sudden tension, a quavering female voice filled the air between the man and me.

"Allen?" the voice called. "Is she coming up?"

"Yes, ma'am," said the man, Allen. "I'll bring her in, like you said." To me, he ordered, "Come on," and led me down a long, carpeted hallway to French doors that opened into a light-bathed bedroom/sitting room, where a pudding of an old woman sat in a sort of decaying splendor in a four-poster canopied bed. There was a messy bed tray in front of her, with a coffee cup and saucer on it and a small china plate with a piece of partly eaten cake spilling its crumbs onto the tray and the bed. Lace curtains had been pulled aside on the leaded glass windows in this room to admit the spring sunshine, and here, the branches of the trees had been cut back to let the light shine in. The woman in bed wore an old-fashioned pink quilted bed jacket, none too clean from the looks of it, and a multitude of sparkly rings on her fingers. I counted five rings without even staring. She had her long white hair piled haphazardly in a bun on top of her head and her earlobes sparkled with dangling earrings that shot green and diamond sparks at me. Several tabloid newspapers were spread out around her and a large TV was blaring a talk show at one side of the bed.

I raised my voice to talk over the noise of the TV.

"I'm Jenny Cain, Mrs. Stewart, from the Hart Foundation?"

She didn't raise her glance from the show on the TV.

"Your son said it would be all right for me to come to meet you this morning—"

She spoke, not to me, but to the silent man behind me.

"Allen, get my son!"

The quavering voice had notes of panic and anger in it. Had I frightened her? Hadn't her son informed her I was coming?

"Yes, ma'am."

I took two steps back, into the space vacated by Allen, hoping to defuse the threat that my presence seemed to pose to her. Behind me, her muscular lackey's quiet footsteps receded quickly down the long hall and then down the front stairs.

"Hurry!" she cried to him.

I said, "Maybe I'd better leave—"

"Yes!" she exclaimed, still not looking at me. "Yes."

I took a chance and said in a rush, "Mrs. Stewart, nobody at the Hart Foundation understands why you're so upset with us or with Carol. All I'm here to do is to try to find out what we did to offend you and to try to make amends. Won't you please—"

She turned and stared at me, looking absolutely wild.

"Do you think I'm *crazy*? Are you as stupid as *she* was?"

Yes! I thought in answer to her first question.

"Stupid?" I asked stupidly.

"You're trying to hurt me! You're trying to manipulate and humiliate an old woman—"

"Mrs. Stewart, for heaven's sakes, I'm not—"

"Just as she tried to do, and I won't have it! Shut up, shut up! Go away, Robin never should have allowed you to come here!" She was horribly upset now, starting to cry and beat on the bedcovers with her fists, like a child having a tantrum. "Allen! Allen! Help me!"

With nothing more to lose, I said, "But what about the ex-convicts, don't you still want to help them?"

"We are already doing quite a lot for them," said a male voice behind me. I turned to find a weary-looking middle-aged man standing there. His prematurely white hair needed trimming; a shock of it fell toward his eyes, which were light blue, like hers. This, I gathered, was Robin Stewart, the minister son. He sounded calm, even wry. "I believe you just met one. Mother's favorite. Allen is a convicted murderer who compounded his error by assaulting another inmate while serving his original term. He was also charged with, but never convicted of, making terroristic threats and attempted rape. There are eight other former convicts living here. Each has a job in the outside world as well as house duties here. Allen, for instance, works at a restaurant in midtown and takes care of the yard." He glanced at the woman in the bed. "And Mother. It's okay, Mom, don't worry about it, calm down now." To me, he said in a softer and apologetic tone, "I'm sorry, but I'd better take you out of here."

"Robin!"

"You want me to call Allen, Mother?"

She nodded violently. "Why did you invite her?"

He smiled slightly. "It seemed like a good idea at the time."

Robin Stewart surprised me then by winking at me and waving me toward the doorway. In the hall, he gently closed the French doors, and we walked together back to the front door. "Did she give you a hard time? I'm sorry. I don't know what kind of bee got up her sleeve about poor Carol, and I'm sorry for the trouble we've caused you." He frowned in a puzzled kind of way. "I thought she *liked* Carol! If you ever figure out what went wrong, I wish you'd let me know."

"I'm sorry, too." I put out my hand for him to shake as we stood on the front porch. "I guess I botched it." I nodded my head toward Allen, who was now at work trimming hedges with electric clippers. "Just out of curiosity, do you ever rehabilitate any of them, Dr. Stewart?"

"I'm not trying to save them," he said in that same calm, wry tone. "If anything, I'm trying to save the rest of us from them." Suddenly, his pale features seemed to tighten as if somebody had pulled back the skin of his scalp. It tightened his smile to a rictus. "I don't like these men. I think they're scum, and I think that getting to live in this house and get counseling and help in finding employment is so much more than they deserve that I can hardly stand to be the one to provide it."

I stared at him. This was hardly what I'd expected.

"But why—"

"For the money."

He smiled, daring me to condemn him.

"I'm not much of a minister, am I?"

"What do you believe in, Dr. Stewart?"

"The future." He raised his gaze to the second floor, where his mother waited for him to send Allen to her, and then he looked frankly into my eyes. "She has never given me a dime's worth of help all my life. She said I needed a college degree, but she wouldn't pay for it and said I had to earn it myself. So I got a minister's mail-order degree. She said I needed to work for a living instead of taking handouts from her. So I found this line of work, which brings in money from the state and invades her precious home and her sense of privacy. It makes her crazy, but she thinks it's worthwhile, I guess, because it makes me look productive." He glanced over at Allen, trimming the hedges. "And it means she gets waited on hand and foot for free. But one day, I fervently hope, she's going to die, and then I'll kick these worthless bums out of my life, and I'll do what I damn well please with all her money." A smile lurking at his lips suggested he was having fun with me. "Disgusting, isn't it?"

"If you say so."

"Disgusting to sit on all this wealth and not even share it with your own child. She won't even leave all her money to me outright. Has to funnel it through some damn foundation like the Hart, so I only get the income, never the principle. Well, it's better than nothing. Now she's looking for a different foundation, now that yours is out. She's a selfish, greedy, disgusting old bitch, and I'd poison her breakfast if I had the nerve to do it."

"Get one of them to do it," I suggested, as dry as he was.

He looked startled and then he laughed. "I've considered it."

"Why'd you invite me over this morning, Dr."—I paused over the title—"Stewart?"

He shrugged. "I'm still curious."

"Me, too," I said, and then I chirped in a sarcastic singsong while I backed down the stairs, "Bye-bye!"

"Call me Robin!"

Not in this lifetime, I thought.

*   *   *

I'd left without calling a cab to take me back into Manhattan, but that was okay—it was a pretty day for walking, and I felt confident I could find my way back to Flatbush Avenue. Once there, I stopped for lunch at a Cambodian restaurant, where I ordered something the waitress could not translate into English for me. It was crunchy, nutty, and delicious, but the taste was totally unfamiliar. I spent an uneasy lunch hour trying to guess what Carol might have said to offend crazy Mrs. Stewart, thinking about ex-cons who were convicted murderers, and also trying to recall if Cambodians eat any animals we don't.

15

ONE-HALF HOUR LATER, I WAS RIDING IN ANOTHER CAB down a street in Greenwich Village when I realized I had nobody to eat dinner with that night. It was a funny thing to think, since I'd just had lunch in Brooklyn. I certainly wasn't hungry for food at the moment, but hungry for company, yes, for somebody (normal) to talk all this over with. Carol. I wanted to talk it all over with Carol. I gazed out the window at all the faces of all those people I would never know, and I wished with all my heart that I might catch a glimpse of her in the crowd.

"So, hey," the cabbie said, "you want to go out tonight?"

I stared at the back of his head. Was I so transparently lonely?

He reached for a card stuck in his visor and handed it back to me. "So, you do, you and the mister, you call me, okay? I'll get you where you want to go. Out to eat. Theater. You name it, I drive it. Anytime. Weeks. Weekends. Don't matter. Here's that theater you wanted. You need a receipt?"

I got out, thinking: Last night I didn't mind being alone, I'd enjoyed coping on my own in the big city. Making my way. Savoring the solitude. Some of it. But now, after spending so much time with strangers—strange strangers, at that—the prospect of dining alone again filled me with a sense of dread. It buffaloed me, this unexpected loneliness. I thought I was used to being alone, what with being single for so long, Geof working late so often, and me off on my own so much. Apparently, I was less well adjusted to it than I knew, or else the very fact of being surrounded by so many faces I didn't know exaggerated my feeling of being apart. There was another word for what I was feeling, but I preferred not to use it: *homesick*.

The Upstage Theater didn't look like much.

There wasn't even a marquee, just posters tacked up on either side of a box office that looked more like an open-air newsstand. *King Leer,* the hand-drawn posters announced, and I laughed. Oh, Lord, if that was an example of the efficiency of this amateur theater group, it was no wonder that Carol had delayed their last payment.

I tried both front doors and found them locked.

Knocking and then pounding produced no response.

Down an alley, I found a side entrance; it even said Stage Door in hand lettering. But it, too, was locked, and still nobody responded to my pounding. Hell's bells. All the way down here, and no way in. Hadn't Damon Calendar told me that morning, on the phone, that they'd be rehearsing all day?

"I thought you were desperate for the money," I muttered to the locked door. I gave it an ill-tempered kick with the toe of my right shoe, but that didn't help, it only scuffed the leather. I decided to try to phone the theater from one of the businesses next door. When I came around to the front again, I saw that my choices were a chains-and-leather shop to the west and a Victorian apparel shop to the east. That looked a mite more friendly, so I went there. I threaded my way through a couple of racks of white frilly dresses that didn't appeal to me any more than chains and leather did, but the young woman behind the counter had a sweet smile.

"Do you know anything about the theater next door?" I asked her. "Like, how can I get into it?"

"Gee, I don't know, they're in and out of there all the time, I assume they use the doors."

I decided she was being ingenuous, not sarcastic.

"All locked, and nobody answers when I knock."

"You want to call them? Use our phone?"

I was hoping she'd offer. I pulled the theater's number out

of my briefcase and actually got somebody on the line: a woman, sounding rushed and distracted. I talked fast. "Hi, I'm Jenny Cain from the Hart Foundation. I'm supposed to get in to see Mr. Calendar, and I'm next door, and I knocked, but I couldn't get anybody to let me in. If I come back, will you let me in, please?"

"No way," she said. "Dress rehearsal."

Like a nervous ingenue, she giggled.

"But Mr. Calendar told me to come down—"

"He must have forgot. Listen, you couldn't get in here if you were William Shakespeare's mother. Especially if you were his mother. If I let you in, Damon'll put my eyes out like Lear's."

"Well, don't do that, but would you tell him—"

"No way! He's directing. We're in *dress* rehearsals," she said, as if any moron but me would grasp the cosmic significance of that unalterable fact. And then she giggled again and hung up on me. The young woman behind the sales counter grimaced sympathetically when she saw me holding the phone and scowling at a dial tone. Since it was a borrowed phone, I didn't slam it down.

"Theater people," I said through clenched jaw, "can be so—"

"Theatrical?" she offered with a helpful air.

That made me smile, and then my glance landed on the lingerie displayed in the glass case directly below my hands. "Oh, how pretty!" I exclaimed, and all of it was, perfectly lovely. The bras and teddies and panties and chemises and slips were wonderfully soft looking and riddled with lacy, sexy, revealing, seductive, provocative little holes and peekaboos. She didn't have to be asked to lay out a richness of exquisite underwear on top of the glass for me to stroke and exclaim over. I imagined my husband also stroking and exclaiming over them and promptly selected a sort of matched set of very bikini white cotton panties that were held together front and back by only slim elastic bands and featured adorable ruffly lace that matched the lacy underwire bra that went with them and the chemise that dipped low at the top and high at the bottom. When I saw the price tags, I gulped.

"Worn by Queen Victoria herself?" I inquired.

She smiled in acknowledgment of the high prices. "Heaven's

no, have you seen pictures of her? I'll bet she wore bloomers as big as horse blankets. These are gorgeous, they'll last a long time if you wash them carefully, and you'll love them."

"*I* am not the point," I confided.

"Then *he'll* love them." But then she quickly added, as if she might have offended me with her casual assumption, "I mean, if it's a he?"

I confirmed it was, and I thought how unlikely it would be ever to hear that question asked in Port Frederick.

She wrapped my lovelies in pretty ivory tissue, which she slipped into a paper bag. I laid it tenderly inside my briefcase. On my way out, we waved at each other, two slightly blushing, lingerie-loving soul sisters.

"Yo, Carol," I said softly. "Nice, huh?"

I had to take a deep breath when I emerged from the cloying atmosphere of Victoriana. A glance in the direction of the chain gang of customers outside the leather store cut the lace in the air quickly enough. A teenage girl flipped me the bird. I flipped it back at her, including the Upstage Theater in my salutation. Well, Carol had wanted to see their dress rehearsal, and now they were having it . . . or were they? Maybe they wouldn't let me in because they didn't want me to know the production wasn't going as they claimed. But if the play wasn't the thing, what was?

It was time to leave the Village and to head uptown to Harlem.

16

I GOT A CAB QUICKLY, BUT THE RIDE DIDN'T LAST LONG.

When I told her what high school I wanted to visit, the driver informed me that she didn't go north of a certain street. "And you're nuts if you do, that blond hair of yours, that briefcase, you'll look like an innocent little bunny wandered into a convention of wolves. What you want to go up there for?"

"It's my job."

"Yeah? Was you, I'd change jobs."

"I'll get out here then."

"Bet you will," she affirmed. We'd moved all of about three yards up the street. "You ought to tip me though for giving *you* a tip, save your life today."

"What's the tip?"

"Don't go."

After three more cab drivers refused to take me to the school where Andrei Bolen ran his Book'Em program for literacy, I searched for a pay phone and found three of them all in a row on a street corner. They were the open-air kind, with plastic walls on only three sides, leaving the front open to anybody's view and hearing. Two were inhabited, so I stepped into the third. It was out of order. I stepped back and started to lean against a building to wait for one of the other two cubicles to get free. Then I thought about how the buildings in this town frequently got used as urinals, and I stopped short before the back of my jacket touched the front of the building.

The phone booth on the left was occupied by a young man who was being lovingly mauled by a young woman who had herself pressed up against his side and who was laying little kisses into his neck. He seemed to be having an argument with the person on the other end of the phone, but between his own sentences, he'd peck a kiss on the young woman's mouth and smile at her. Then he'd go back to arguing on the phone. Frown and argue, peck and smile, frown and argue, peck and smile. Looked like a pretty enjoyable routine to me and one that could last all day.

In the middle cubicle, there was a woman about my age who was also arguing with somebody on the other end of the phone, only there was nobody nearby to coax a smile from her. Her argument kept escalating as I stood there trying not to listen. Then I realized that people who yelled into public telephones probably didn't care much about privacy, so I frankly stared and eavesdropped. What the hell, I wasn't in any hurry; and the longer I stood there, the longer I could delay going up to Harlem.

"You tell that moron you live with not to hang up on me again!" screamed the woman in the middle. She banged down the receiver and then stood there staring at it while I willed her away from it. I couldn't see her face, just her long, curly brown hair and the back of her nice gray business suit. She wore hose and tennis shoes, so she must be on a late lunch hour, I figured, and she'd tucked her high heels under her desk before she left her office. Surely, I'd get the phone now. They'd hung up on her, she'd hung up on them, what more was there to say? But no, she stood there, visibly vibrating, and then she grabbed the receiver as if it were somebody's throat she wanted to throttle, rammed more change into the slot, and punched in numbers as if they were eyes she was poking out.

"You put him back on the line!" she screamed this time, apparently at the "moron" who'd hung up on her last time. I felt the moron might have the highest IQ in the crowd, and here was another chance for her to prove that by hanging up again and giving me a chance at the phone. And then Gray Suit screamed, "Don't tell me I'm out of control, I am not fucking out of control!" At which point, the moron must have done it again, God bless her, because Gray Suit & Curly Hair whirled around, receiver still in her hand, and now I could see her face. She was perfectly ordinary looking, except for the red blotches around her mouth, cheeks, and eyes. Her mouth hung open, as if all the furious words she'd been ready to discharge at the moron were spilling out on the sidewalk at her feet. She didn't notice me or anything else for that matter; she was intent on her inner visions, which probably included death by drive-by killing, disfigurement and dismemberment, and murder for hire. She dropped the receiver as if it were trash and then strode, seemingly full of resolve and purpose, away from the booth, stepped over the curb, and walked two paces out into the street.

I was fascinated by now: What would she do next?

The street in which she stood was empty of moving vehicles, because a red light had stopped the one-way traffic coming our way. Gray Suit stood by herself in the quiet street for a moment or two. Her arms hung at her sides. She faced the street, but I had a feeling she wasn't really seeing it. And suddenly I could feel exactly what she was thinking: *Oh, God, what do I do now?* She'd burned her bridges. Called one friend a moron. Screamed at the other one. Hung up on them. Now, here she was, abrim with the energy of her fury, but there was no place for her to go with it. I watched her sway a little on her feet, perhaps dizzied by the awful apocalyptic wave of realization that might now be sweeping over her: *Oh, shit, what have I done?* Or, maybe it was: *I'll kill them, I hate them!*

The light at the end of the block changed, the traffic started our way, but still she remained directly in their path, and they were coming fast out of the gate, as New York drivers do, like impatient horses. I realized she was facing a choice, right here, in this New York minute. How upset was she? How forsaken did she feel? Or desperate or humiliated or vengeful or alone? Enough to wait until the last minute and then to take one fatal step *forward?*

Here was the death membrane again, right in front of me.

It was everywhere, not just covering open windows, but also in the eyes of convicted murderers you happened to meet, in cars just a hand's length away from you, in empty streets where hookers beckoned, even standing right here minding my own business (kind of), where anything could happen, where I could *choose* death in any number of ways. Death was more out in the open here. More in your face. *Here I am, take me or leave me, but you* will *notice me,* death said in New York City.

A mere second ahead of the first car, she stepped back.

Then she started walking down the sidewalk away from me, into a future I'd never see. Would it contain the moron and the person the moron lived with? Would they forgive her? Would she forgive them? I'd never know.

"This city is so damned *personal,*" I muttered.

I stepped toward the phone booth she had vacated only to discover that a middle-aged man had stepped into it ahead of me. Finally, five minutes later, after he ended a conversation that seemed to consist of an argument over ballpoint pens, and after which he plunked down the receiver so hard it bounced and fell off the hook, *then* the telephone was mine, and I used it to call Patty Vinitsky at her law office.

"It's not five o'clock," she snapped. "I thought I told you, I don't do charity work before five."

"Don't hang up!"

"Hang up? Why would I hang up?"

"Never mind. Just tell me how to get to Harlem to meet Andrei Bolen if no cab will take me there. Better yet, tell me why I should want to go where no cabbie will take me."

"Call a for-hire car. I'll give you a number of a company I use."

"You didn't answer the important question: Why should I?"

"Look, Jenny, Andrei goes to work there every day, why shouldn't you go once? It's not that bad once you get there. In fact, there are some pretty nice neighborhoods, I've got friends who live in Harlem. Maybe not where *you're* going, but still . . . just have the car pull up in front, I'll call Andrei and alert him you're coming, and he'll send somebody out to escort you into the building."

"What is it, a war zone?"

"Of course, don't you read the papers about public schools? Guns, drugs, gangs. That's why we need Andrei's literacy program. Listen, go. Trust me. How's everything else going?"

"Let me put it this way, Pat: This trip to Harlem may turn out to be the high point of my day. Mrs. Stewart hates me, hates Carol, hates the foundation, and she would probably hate you if she knew you, no offense. I am standing near the Upstage Theater, where I pounded on every door until my knuckles broke, and nobody ever let me in, in spite of the fact that what'shisname knew I was coming. I have an appointment with Dr. and Mrs. Lloyd at their home this evening, which I will probably never live to keep."

"I was hoping for better than this." Her tone was peevish and disappointed, but I was disinclined to feel guilty about it. "Well, at least you'll get the site evaluation done for Andrei's grant, and we'll get that in the works."

"Four cabbies refused to take me, Pat. *Four* of them."

"So, they were probably all fresh off the boat from Iraq; they wouldn't take you because they don't know the way and they can't read maps in English. You'll be all right. You'll live. I'm telling you, trust me."

"Go with me?"

"I've got clients all afternoon."

"Pat, I'm feeling very small-town girlish right at this moment. Very naive. Very out-of-towner. Very not–New York. Very conspicuous, very *white*. I have black friends, you understand, but they are not *here*. I am *alone*."

"Call this company," and she read me a number.

"Call my husband if I don't come back."

"Give me a break! Do you know what the odds are against one foundation losing two directors in one month?"

"They're improving by the minute," I said and hung up, that being the time-honored tradition at this phone booth. Against every ounce of good judgment I possessed, I called the car-for-hire company. They promised, after only a slight hesitation and a credit card number, to send a driver for me within thirty minutes. I spent that at a coffee shop near the pay phones, figuring that I'd need the caffeine if I had to run for my life. This is not prejudice, I kept telling myself, this is Harlem, where you are going in your business suit with your pale face and your blond hair and your look of unmerited prosperity, so why don't you just wear a sign that says Mug Me?

Perversely, I wished I had some of Mrs. Golding's baked

goods to go with my cafe au lait. I thought sourly as I waited to meet my fate: So where's a good obsessive/compulsive when you really need one? By the time a nondescript gray sedan pulled up and double-parked in front of the pay phones and a tall black man got out of the driver's seat and stared around as if he was looking for somebody, I was jumpy as a cat on caffeine.

17

Desolation. It grew like a warped garden spreading north into the upper reaches of Manhattan. Everything grew backward here: It was the thorns that prospered instead of the roses. It didn't happen all at once, it was slow, block by block, neighborhood by neighborhood, but then it picked up speed like our cab did, until the decay was rampant, like an overgrowth of strangling vines.

The sidewalks sparkled with broken glass.

"We've lost eight drivers," my own driver said out of the blue, speaking into the silence that had come over us as we moved north of midtown. That was the thing about New York City, as Patty Vinitsky had hinted the first day I met her: It was a continent; not just an island, but a complete continent broken up into countries that were so different from one another they might as well have raised their own flags, opened embassies, traded diplomats, and officially declared wars and peace. I was barely listening when my driver added, "In the last two months alone."

"They quit?" I asked, not paying attention.

He snorted, and suddenly I woke up to the derision in the sound. "Quit? Yeah, they quit. They quit living. They were killed. In their cars. Just like this one. By their passengers."

He threw me a glance in his rearview mirror and must have seen my startled expression. "That's how it goes, you know? You never know who you're picking up, what kind of crackhead or weirdo. We don't carry no money, they told you that when you called?"

I nodded so he could see me in the mirror.

"Right, that's why they made you give 'em a credit card number. So you know I don't have no cash. That's what it says on the outside of our cars now. Driver Carries No Cash."

"You carry your life in your hands."

"You got that right. They was stabbed, a couple of them, but mostly shot. Back of the head." I sensed the death membrane shimmering between us, separating the front seat from the back, and how easily it could be ripped open by the blade of a knife or a bullet. "Side of the head, execution like. They were mostly going uptown, like now. I almost didn't take this ride, except the dispatcher, she told me you was a woman, you sounded like a educated white gal, maybe a outtatowner, and when she asked you, how many in your party, you said it was just you, so I figure, you got no man with you. Hey, you packin' a pistol in that briefcase of yours?"

"No."

And then his paranoia infected me like a sudden onslaught of the flu, and I felt my face grow feverish with fear. Why was I telling this man how unprotected I was? He had nothing to fear from me, that was the message he sought and had so easily obtained from me. But what if I had something to fear from him? Now he knew I was a woman alone, going into a neighborhood that was not her own, carrying no gun for protection. *Nice going, Jenny,* I thought, *play right into his hands.* I slid closer to the door, so I could throw myself out of it if anything happened to make me feel some urgent need to escape from his car.

"We'll be all right," he said. "I'll get you there."

As I gazed out the windows, I thought I could see the membrane glistening everywhere: in the cracks of broken windows and the alleys behind the buildings. It draped itself over the street corner trash cans, where groups of men were gathered, and over the too young mothers carrying their babies, and it trailed out wispy veins behind the old people clutching their belongings to their chests. You didn't have to look for it here, you didn't even have to make a conscious choice to step through it; it came looking for you, lived with you, made you step around it, over it, and cross the street to avoid it, every minute, every day.

"Here's the school," he said, pulling to a stop.

I looked up and saw a building with windows broken out, asphalt buckled on the playgrounds, weeds growing where the asphalt wasn't. Two utterly stripped cars had been abandoned in the center of the street, so that traffic had to navigate around them. I heard somebody yelling but couldn't make out the words, only the feeling of rage behind the voice. There were clumps of kids hanging around outside the building and the half-torn-down chain-link fence that surrounded it. Some of them were smoking cigarettes—or joints, from the look of the way they held and sucked them. Others stared at the car, my driver, me.

"You going in there by yourself?" he asked me.

"Will you go with me?"

"Nope."

Once he had deposited me on the curb in front of the school, he drove quickly away from me. To my relief, I saw an armed police officer walking toward me, coming from the direction of the front doors. I watched some of the kids put out—or stroll away with—their smokes. The cop was looking for something or somebody: me?

A nearby group of black teenage boys, all wearing similar colors, shifted their positions slightly as they stared at me. One of them started to whistle "God Bless America." When I recognized the tune, I laughed. A couple of them grinned back at me, and one of them called out, "You lost, little darlin'? What're you doin' up here, you want me to take you home, sweet thing? I'll protect you." He grinned at his pals. "She looks like she needs some protection, what you think? Like a nice little Mercedes car, you know?" He looked back at me, all smiles. "You want me to wash your windows, darlin'? I won't let nobody smash your windows, nor nothin' else, you know? How 'bout it, you come on with me, I'll protect you, get you away from these other bad dudes."

His pals hooted and shoved him in my direction.

The cop walked up and placed himself between me and them. "She's got protection," he said, unsmiling, not amused at what appeared to be edgy play. Play with an attitude. "And I'm it, assholes." He patted the huge gun in the holster at his hip. "Smash this, why don't you? Wash this for me. I'll break something for you. Get back to class if that's where you belong, or get the hell gone. What're you doin' hanging around outside here? Get your asses movin'."

They didn't budge. They didn't laugh either. But their stares followed the cop and me into the building. I could feel the curiosity and the heat of their regard on our backs. When we stepped inside, I turned to look back: The one who'd spoken to me saluted with the third finger of his right hand, but I couldn't tell if he meant it for me or for the cop. I heard his friends laugh, and a couple of them slapped his shoulders, and then they casually began to move away from the fence.

I turned to say to the cop, "I'm here to—"

"I know what you're here for. I'm taking you there now."

"Thank you."

I wanted to pepper him with questions, to learn about this place, this high school, this armed camp where boys and girls came to learn that the capital of Afghanistan is Kabul and the square root of four is two and that it's *i* before *e* except after *c*. But he looked tough and as angry as if he'd been born scowling. I walked a pace behind him in silence. It didn't take me long to see why he discouraged chitchat. As his head swiveled like a gun in a turret, I realized he was scanning for trouble. He was a spy in enemy territory. Searching for gun emplacements. Alert to suspicious movement of personnel and matériel. The racket pouring out of some of the classrooms was unbelievable: loud talking, raucous laughter, even singing. How could anybody learn anything?

He deposited me in front of a door in a dingy basement of the school, giving the frosted glass a double rap with his knuckles that made the glass rattle in its frame. Then he walked off, back to his unenviable job, leaving me standing alone in the deserted hallway lined with broken lockers. When I opened the door, a thirtyish white man seated at a long table looked up at me quizzically and then gave a welcoming nod.

"Mme. Cain!"

BUT I WOULDN'T WANT TO *DIE* THERE

Andrei Bolen was thin and short, with shoulder-length black hair pulled back into a ponytail and magnetic black eyes set in an attractively saturnine face that lit up charmingly when he smiled. When he spoke, it was with a French accent that would have melted the socks off any living heterosexual female and quite a few men. Instantly, I got a much better understanding of Pat Vinitsky's attraction to this . . . project.

He jumped to his feet and pulled out a chair for me so that I could sit next to him.

"You are here!" He appeared rapturous, making my appearance sound like the Second Coming. "How wonderful! And how beautiful you are! I hope you don't object to my saying so, one never knows what American women will object to . . . but Patricia didn't warn me that I would have to keep my heart from jumping out of my chest when you appeared suddenly like this, like Aphrodite!"

Good grief, I thought.

"Hello," I said.

He sat back down but leaned passionately toward me.

"Now we will save the children," he said, "now we will teach them all to read, now they will get jobs and raise families and move out of this terrible place and be human beings again instead of beasts." He made a distinctly Gallic sound of contempt and raised his glance to the ceiling to indicate the people in the classrooms above us. I scooted my chair back, not much liking the crack about "beasts." The people I'd seen had looked exactly like human beings to me.

"Mr. Bolen, Andrei, what are you doing . . . here?"

"I have a mission." Indeed, I could see the zeal in his eyes. "I saw these schools on television at home in France, I was an instructor in a seminary, and I said, There is my mission, like the missionaries of old who went to Africa to offer salvation to the native tribes. I can do that, I said to myself, I can save them. I have the skills, the energy, I have the mission. So I just came"—he shrugged, so Gallic, so attractive—"and offered myself to the principal and I said, Use me, I will charge you nothing, I will take nothing from you, I will only give to you, give and give and give until I am depleted if that is what is required of me. And she, saintly woman, she was finally convinced, she gave me this room and she said, Do what you can. And so, I began recruiting students!"

I regarded him with disfavor.

I hated working with fanatics. They made it so hard to get the facts on which to base a decision about giving them money, and frankly, I didn't trust them. I didn't trust this man, his story, or his wild enthusiasm. I didn't even trust that anybody could actually do what he wanted to do. And I *really* didn't like his referring to the people upstairs as "beasts" and then, obliquely, as "native tribes." This man was, as far as I could see, the equivalent of a European disease. He was smallpox. He was bad news. He was going to have a whale of a lot to demonstrate to me before I recommended one penny of Hart Foundation money for him.

Right on, Carol, I thought, remembering her files.

I looked him in the eyes and said, "Okay, prove it."

He appeared delighted to do so and promptly started pulling out papers to show to me. I looked down at them and then back up at him. "Very impressive," I said, "but there's one problem. These records are all in French."

"But they are true in any language!"

I laughed, really laughed, until there were tears in my eyes. It was a great release of tension, and he—damned phony— laughed right along with me as if he got the joke. When I quieted down, I closed up to him, boarded up like a storefront window with a sign that said Closed.

"Okay, Andrei, sum it up for me. Tell me in English the secret of your success."

He smiled flirtatiously at me. "I pay them."

"Who?"

"The students. I pay them to learn to read. You will give me money so I can give them money so they will be literate and save their lives."

"You pay them."

"It is very direct, Mme. Cain."

"It is very impossible, Mr. Bolen."

He looked shocked and stricken. "But Patricia said—"

"Yes, well, we'll see." I had visions of Hart Foundation cash pouring directly into his trouser pockets and never coming back out again. We'd never know that for sure, of course, as all of the proof would be written down in French! "This has been *trés* interesting. I'll get back to you. Thank you for your time."

Just as I was leaving, a black teenage boy pushed the door open and walked in. He sat down on the other side of the table without acknowledging the presence of the adults in the room.

"Where can I find a phone to call a cab?" I asked Bolen.

"Principal's office," the boy said.

"Will you walk me there?" I asked the teacher.

He pulled back his head like a French chicken and said, "*Mais, porquoi?*"

"*Why?*" the teenager interjected, easily translating what his teacher had just said. "Because she might get killed between here and there, man, that's *why*. Or if you don't like killed, how about raped. And if that don't appeal to you, try the fact that she might get stripped of that briefcase. That's *porquoi*, man!" He stared at me, then tossed aside the book he had picked up and had started to read. "Come on, I'll walk you."

I saw that the book he set aside was *The Prince* and that he had opened it to a page toward the middle. As we walked up the stairs to the first floor, I said, "So what do you think of Machiavelli?"

"I think he'd have made a great drug dealer," the boy said without missing a beat or looking at me. "Fit right into this neighborhood. Make it big. Manipulate his way into money. Lie his way out of anything. It's all politics, man, even criminals, even school, it's all politics."

"But you're reading it."

"Yeah, I'm reading it."

"And he's paying you to do that?"

He looked at me then, cocking an eyebrow. "Beats working."

"You think it'll get you a better job someday?"

His laugh was serious and derisive. "Who's got a someday? I don't give a fuck about no someday. I only care about this day, and this day I need some coins. Mr. Bolen, if he's dumb enough to pay me to read his stupid books, then I'm going to take his money."

"But you don't think the book is so stupid?"

We'd reached the high school principal's office by then. And for the first time, the kid's face cracked into expression; it was a half smile full of whole knowledge. "Nah, that Machiavelli, like I said, he was a pretty smart dude. I wouldn't mind being like him myself." He loped away, leaving me to think: Now there was a message of mixed blessings if I ever heard one. Still, I stared at his long, lean retreating back, and I wondered if that sign on the boarded-up store of my brain ought to have read Closed Mind.

Carol and I had usually had the same instincts: Were we both wrong about Bolen?

"I'll call the car for you myself. What company do you want?"

The principal, Barbara Moore, was a big woman, easily six feet tall in her low heels, and built top-heavy like a fighter. She had a gently pugnacious face with a lot of humor in it and the biggest bags I'd ever see under a woman's eyes. They looked like she'd need Jed, my doorman, to carry them. I took as instant a liking to this fiftyish black principal as I had taken an instant dislike to her volunteer in the basement.

"How about an armored car?" she suggested.

"Then I'm not just being a white suburban paranoid?"

She smiled wearily. "Oh, you may be that, too, I wouldn't know. But it's appropriate to feel endangered here. It is dangerous. It is appropriate to take precautions. Next time, you might want to dress down for one thing—"

"I didn't know I was coming so soon, or I'd have changed—"

"You'll never camouflage yourself, not unless you put a hood over that hair, but you could look less Park Avenue, less like a target."

"I don't think there will be a next time."

She was making the call to the car company, and when that was completed, she said, "Why not? Don't you like us?"

"It's Bolen."

"Andrei? What's not to like? It works, you know, his program. Book'Em works. Kids who never read before are picking up books for the first time. The kid who showed you in here, his grades are picking up. I wouldn't say that I believe Book'Em will work the miracles Andrei claims it will, but that's just Andrei, blowin' smoke."

"It's not *all* just smoke?"

"He didn't show you his stats?"

"They're in *French*, Mrs. Moore!"

"Barbara. The numbers aren't. The man knows what he's doing and does what he says. If I could clone him and put one of him in every classroom, I'd do it today."

"But *pay* them to read?"

"You got a better idea?"

"What's he been using for money till now?"

"Donations." I saw an amused glint in her eyes.

"Churches? Other foundations?"

"From the French people." The glint grew to a near smile. "He raised money from people back home to give to disadvantaged students in the United States."

"Good God," I said.

She grinned outright. "God is good, as you say."

"So I guess you want us to fund the program."

"I'd recommend that if you don't, he and I will kill you."

I smiled, taking it as a joke.

"I'm not kidding," she told me. "We need help, and he's part of it. Your foundation better give him the money, or I promise you I'll send a couple of my kids down to break your arms." Again, she smiled, and again, I assumed she was joking. "We breed psychopaths up here, you know. Or sociopaths if you prefer. I can supply examples of most any variety of mental or emotional or spiritual aberration that appeals to you. This is a laboratory for creating violence and ignorance, a culture, a mold growing wild in a petri dish. And unless we find an antidote, I promise you it will spread; we can infect a whole population with our virulent bacteria, just you watch and see if we don't, and then nice, effective little programs like Book'Em are going to be useless. It's not hopeless now. Not yet."

"May I call you later to talk more?"

"No." She sighed deeply. "I have said all I have the energy to say to you. Talk to Andrei, talk to his pupils if they'll give you the time of day, and judge for yourself, but don't waste my time on it. It's clear as glass to me, it's obvious, it's right. And you're the fool, like Carol Margolis was, God rest her soul, if you don't see it my way and Ms. Vinitsky's." She gave me a look to remind me that my boss agreed with her. "Just do it, and don't bother me anymore with it. It's nothing personal. It's just that I got no time for you. Look, another time, another part of town, we could meet for lunch, have coffee, maybe a drink, discover we like each other, maybe start a friendship, two normal women, leading normal lives downtown. Well, my life is not normal by any standards you ever heard of. I got Uzi submachine guns for the first bell and I got fornication in the stairwells for lunch, I got cussing in the very air I breathe, and I got despair and fury all around me. I am hanging on to hope by the skin of my fingers. I have to exercise my smile muscles to get them to work. I got no time for friends, especially new ones. Heck, I have no time for lunch, for coffee. I only have room in my heart for the terror that's growing there."

She leaned toward me, even more passionate than Andrei Bolen.

"Somebody's got to do something to help me! And you're one of the privileged somebodies who's going to do it." She checked her watch, an inexpensive looking thing with a huge face on it. "Your car should be here."

As we walked together to the front door of the school, Barbara Moore said to me, "Somebody said that people who have been extraordinarily disadvantaged should get extraordinary advantages for a while, just to enable them to catch up. I believe that. And this ain't no extraordinary thing we're asking, just a little money for just a little more literacy. Come on, I'll walk you on out to the car, keep you from getting mugged between here and there."

I stared back at her as the car pulled away from the littered curb. She stood on the broken asphalt like a figure out of mythology, a big, strong, tough goddess, Artemis in a cotton dress, a black Hera—angry, powerful, jealous of her turf, and desperate to hang on to it. She was Artemis astride a war zone, refusing to leave until she'd battled down the enemies of righteousness or been slain herself. I wasn't exaggerating the woman's aura of power; if anything, I was understating it.

In the front seat, the driver said, "We lost eight drivers in the last couple of months, you know that?"

Yes, I said, I knew that.

18

I SLIPPED UP TO THE APARTMENT AND THEN INTO A COMFORT-
able pair of sweats and a T-shirt, ready to put my feet up. But
I discovered that I couldn't sit still in my pretty, clean rooms.
Two different worlds, this afternoon and now. I felt cooped up,
wired, upset.

And I still didn't trust Andrei Bolen.

Distractedly, I killed some time by taking my new lingerie
out of my briefcase and lovingly sliding it into Carol's underwear drawer. So pretty. A thrill of sheer sexual anticipation
coursed through me as I imagined Geof's first glimpse. I pulled
out a pair of white socks, decidedly unsexy, went to the closet
for my tennis shoes, and went out for a walk.

The walk got faster and faster until I, who never moved faster
than a brisk trot, was running, running, running down the paths
of Riverside Park, past the cages, the caged basketball players,
the caged handball players, the caged children, the caged babies. Cages, cages, cages. Did they get used to this, I asked
myself, did they ever really get used to it, or did it gradually
just drive them all crazy, and was it that craziness that was the
real secret generator at the heart of the energy that poured
through this city? *Let me out of here!* I thought in pounding
rhythm to my feet. *Take this city away from me, and put it*

out of its misery. I understood why Geof hated it, why he loathed to come here. I got it, I got it. *I want to go home,* I thought. I flung myself at the trunk of a tree, gasping for breath, dizzied by the unaccustomed exertion.

"You ought to take it slower," a voice said.

I looked up and saw a young black woman standing by my tree. She smiled. She was wearing a pretty jogging suit of polished yellow cotton. Her hair was cornrowed into a French braid, and her fingernails were long and crimson. Surreptitiously, I checked mine: not turning black with fungus yet. She said in a brusque voice, "You'll make yourself sick. You haven't been running long, I'll bet. I mean, you haven't made it a habit yet. Start slow, build up, take your time, enjoy it. Don't get shin splints or a stress fracture. And, God, get the right shoes, girl! And don't run yourself out of breath. You can be too eager and ruin it for yourself." She patted my shoulder, then started off to renew her own run, looking cool and pretty. "Stay with it, you'll love it!"

I couldn't even speak to say thank you or what was more likely on my mind: *Damn bossy New Yorkers! Thought they knew everything. Thought they were smarter, hipper, braver than anybody else.* If she'd looked back, though, she'd have seen me grin in her direction, raising an exhausted arm to wave. Bossy like relatives, that's what they were, all of them bossing each other around, roughly, affectionately. *Godspeed!* I sent the wish after her. *And thanks.* It took me several minutes more to regroup my body and my emotions. Finally, I limped back to my building. The parents and babies in the smallest cages seemed to be having a fine time. The men in the basketball cage were sweating, pushing, joking loudly with each other. There was vitality in the air. *Life.* I breathed it in greedily. I was going to need it: My first day at work for the Hart Foundation wasn't even over yet.

When I went to cross at the light, I encountered the runner again.

"Why do people run?" I asked her, honestly curious.

She was jogging in place. "Why did you, back then?"

"Getting something out of my system, I guess."

"Not me. I'm running away from home." She grinned. "Three kids and a husband. This is the only privacy I get all day. That's why I run. See ya." She took off again before the light changed, leaving me to limp home, wondering, "Why did *you* run, Carol?"

And why, oh, God, why didn't you run faster?

I took a hot shower and got cleaned up for dinner.

Before I went out, I knocked on my landlady's door, thinking I'd speak to her about Mr. Daley Bread and the hall lights. Nobody answered, so I walked back down the hall to try Jed's door.

"My husband's arriving late tomorrow night," I told him. "Will you be on duty? Will you let him go on up?"

"Sure, no problem."

He was leaning against his hands, which were propped against his doorsill. I was standing downwind of his beer intake.

"You're sure somebody will be here to let him in?"

"Hey!" He bounced back, looking wounded, offended, and he said loudly, "I said I'd do it, didn't I?"

"Sorry," I said, trying to soothe him. "I know you will."

"Damn straight!" He shot a fist into the air and pretended to shadowbox with me all the way out both exit doors. "I'm on the job! Jed's your man!"

"My man" was higher than the Chrysler building.

I got into my umpteenth cab of the day and thought: *Is everybody crazy in this city, or is it just me?*

After my solitary dinner, I was due at the Central Park South condominium of Dorothy and Dr. Malcolm Lloyd. They were the couple who were angry because the Hart Foundation was giving their money to a South Bronx gardening project instead of to the controversial, fraud-riddled Black Company.

On my way, I directed the driver on a detour.

He didn't want to go, until I told him our destination was the Growth Fund, which was the name of the garden.

"Oh, right, I know that place," he said. "Real nice, that garden."

When we got there, what I saw under streetlights was a full city block truck garden surrounded by a chain-link fence that appeared to be at least seven feet tall and was topped by several strands of barbed wire.

"Used to be tenements here," the cabbie offered. "Look at it now."

"What happened to the buildings?"

"What ever happens? I dunno. Fire, maybe. It happens. Then nobody wants to renovate. Nobody wants to buy it. It commences to cave in. The city has too much goin' on, doesn't force the owners to fix it. They start gettin' bad publicity. Then the owners get smart, practically give it away as a tax write-off, public relations gimmick, like this here. You ought to see it in the summer, tomatoes big as baseballs, cabbages big as your head. I don't mind drivin' by here. In fact, I like it. Seeing the people out workin' in it, middle of the damned city. Kids, too. If you walk up to the fence, sometimes they'll give you something, a carrot, nice sweet bell pepper, it's nice. All organic, too. And they sell stuff on Saturdays and Sunday mornings, clear up to Halloween. Then it's pumpkins. Squash and stuff. I like thinkin' about it. Thing like this, where it's at, kind of gives you hope, you know what I mean?"

At first, there didn't appear to be much to see.

I could easily have confused it with any deserted city block.

But there was something about the lack of litter on the sidewalks around it. Something about the fence, how straight and correct it stood, no links broken, no lines sagging, no gates hanging loose. Something about the number of padlocks I glimpsed on the gate. And then my eyes adjusted to the night, and I saw the lovely rows within the fence, the little stakes and beribboned posts, the arbors and the tool shed. And something else.

"Do you see somebody in there?" I asked.

The cabbie rolled down his window, stared. "Oh, yeah, right over against the shed. They keep a pretty good guard out here. I imagine that's one of them."

I could see the man more clearly now. Yes, seated on the bare ground with his back against the door of the shed, he was barely visible until I saw a small beam of light and realized he was holding a flashlight and that its beam was captured and

held in the pages of a book. I strained to see, for some reason
desiring to know what he was reading: It was a hardcover from
a library, from the looks of it, but I couldn't possibly make out
the cover.

I stuck my head out and yelled.

"Excuse me . . . what are you reading?"

He looked up, then quickly extinguished his light. He was
no longer visible to me, but his voice carried to the curb as he
enunciated carefully, so that I caught every word, *"Possessing
the Secret of Joy!"*

I drew in my breath at the lovely coincidence of it: It was
the very novel by Alice Walker that I'd been reading back home
in Port Frederick. I called back to him, *"Me, too!"*

"No kidding?" said the cab driver.

"Good!" came the reply, which I took to be a favorable re-
view of the book and of my reading habits.

"Ain't that somethin'?" asked my cabbie. "You and him reading the same damned book. Is this an amazing town or what?
Is it any good? The book, I mean? What'd he call it? My wife,
she reads a lot. Novels, that kind of thing, you know."

"It's very good." I leaned back in the seat, feeling unaccount-
ably pleased with myself. I repeated the title, which he wrote
down on a blank taxi receipt form. I thought about the fictional
child Tashi, taken by her mother to hide on a farm after the
horrible death of her sister. It all seemed connected, somehow,
that book about Africa, written by an African-American female
novelist, being read by the black American male gardener. And
me. Passing on the word to the wife (of unknown color) of the
white taxi driver who loved the garden in the black neighborhood. Why did it make me feel so good, so sentimental? What
was the "it" of which we were all pieces?

"We can go now," I said. "Thanks."

"You're very welcome."

I craned my neck for a last look at the vast, dark, enclosed
garden. The cab driver was right, it gave you hope. It was
somebody's dream come true. It was why I was in my line of
work. "There's a clue here, Jenny," I said to myself, "about
what you might want to be when you grow up."

I gawked at the night sights as we moved south.

I suspected that this was what I had to convince the Lloyds

of. Had either of them actually ever seen the garden? Surely, it would be well-nigh irresistible, and maybe I'd just have to drag them down there. And so, it was on a wave of rosy sentiment and optimism that I sailed past the doorman of their elegant condominium building on Central Park South and onto the elevator with elevated hopes for Saving the Day. Why, any reasonable person would see things my way . . .

I took one look at Dr. Malcolm Lloyd's face and had an instant vision of ancient grudges festering. This man did not appear to possess the secret of joy. Except for the blackness of his skin, I could imagine him as a feudal lord in the north of Scotland, ruddy of skin and rough of temperament, a boon to his king because of his reckless courage and his sharp intelligence, but a prickly, dangerous nettle all the same. You could see that this man craved battle; it was in his body and eyes. He thirsted for drama. I glimpsed long-held resentments, the kind that span generations and go back centuries in families where offense is taken easily and forgiveness comes hard. He was past middle age, but he looked burly and vigorous, as if his hatreds nourished him as blood does a vampire bat. He was of a good height, although he carried his wide shoulders hunched in over his wide chest, as if he were hovering over a blistering campfire of grudges that he carried in his heart. He had closely trimmed silver and black hair, and a full beard and moustache, also shot with silver, which lent him even more of the appearance of an ancient, battle-scarred, and fatally proud feudal lord of some windswept, godforsaken castle on a high, blustery cliff above a northern sea.

He'd been a surgeon, Patty Vinitsky had said.

It was a horrifying thought: I envisioned huge blades in his hands—wood-handled axes, machetes, swords—and gaping wounds with flowing blood and Dr. Malcolm Lloyd standing over the helpless bodies of his patients, roaring his sovereignty over the operating room and all within range of him.

All this within thirty seconds of meeting him.

Rarely had any human being made such an immediate and

dramatic impression on me. Or, maybe, I'm imagining some of it in hindsight because now I know what was to come.

If he was the blustering lord of the manor, Dorothy Lloyd was the epitome of the lady of it, as delicate and finely mannered as her husband was gruff and rough. I could easily picture Mrs. Lloyd in tightly bodiced, beautifully embroidered flowing robes of forest green velvet or a deep velvet blue like a sky at the close of twilight. In fact, she was wearing a loose, filmy dress, a delicate brown and black leopard print, whose skirts swept the floor when she moved. She had a slight British accent—I learned she had been born in Nigeria—and she seemed to handle him with the constant wariness and nervous grace of a lion tamer.

Their apartment was a spectacular backdrop for this remarkable looking couple. It appeared to be incredibly expensive and elegant, but that wasn't what made it eyepopping. I saw only the living and dining rooms, which led out onto a balcony that overlooked Central Park. The walls of those two rooms were covered in what looked like a deep, glowing brown leather but, she told me, was actually lacquer. "I made them apply ten coats, until they got the effect I wanted," she said, and her husband waved his hand scoffingly, as if such astonishing interior decorating was too mundane to mention. The floors were a glowing brown marble speckled with black flecks. I'd never seen marble of that color or quality in a private home, and combined with the effect of the walls, it gave me the feeling of floating in a vat of the richest chocolate. They had what looked to me like a fabulous collection of African artifacts—masks, sculpture, lances, shields, and the like—displayed in niches along the walls and arranged so that each piece looked as if it floated in warm, golden light. The furniture, too, was deep brown and black and made of the softest, most buttery leather. The central seating arrangement of four long squared-off sofas was softly lit from above by the same golden glow that illuminated the objects in the walls. The effect was astonishing: All was dark, except for the art along the perimeters and the people in the center. The lighting brought their darker complexions to glowing life, giving even Dr. Lloyd a fierce beauty, while I felt as if my Nordic skin stood out like a white shirt under an ultraviolet lamp. After a few moments in the living room with them, I realized that it was more than simply a feeling that I was sitting under a spotlight, it was that in that setting I felt like . . . prey.

It made me uneasy, uncomfortable, and I felt sure they knew that. I didn't even bother to wonder if they had done it on purpose. It seemed obvious they had designed their home to make black people feel an at-homeness that transcended this city, this year, that reached as far back, farther and deeper and more meaningfully back, than my sense of northern European-ness extended for me. They were black. Their causes were black causes. Their art was African. They defined their identity by another continent, another age than mine, and I visited it at their sufferance. Odd, then, that my inner vision saw them in a cold and ancient northern court rather than in a royal line of their actual lineage.

"You've taken Carol's place?" Mrs. Lloyd inquired.

That simple question was a shock in that complex setting.

We were seated on separate couches, three points of a square. Behind her, the park was a black hole surrounded by the glittering lights of the apartments lining Central Park east and west. Behind him, a dark carved statue of a tribesman stared at me from eyes of stone. I explained the situation at the foundation. Mrs. Lloyd expressed regret at Carol's death, and the doctor sat hunched and silent during the women's polite duet.

Then he lost patience with us.

"I *despise* your insipid little gardens of triviality!"

I glanced at her for help, but she sat as still as one of their dark statues, moving only to adjust her skirts or to fiddle quietly with a button on her bodice.

"Have you actually seen the garden?" I ventured.

She shook her head in an almost imperceptible movement, as if she didn't want him to notice.

"Do you think our gift of our money to the Hart Foundation was a trivial gesture?" he demanded, nearly shouting. "Is it meaningless to you people, do you think we gave it to you to squander? I don't give a *damn* about your green beans and petunias! How dare you employ my money to purchase trowels and potting soil to benefit a few greedy little people when the

same money could be used to change the world, to revolution-
ize this country, to bring honor to my family?"

Finally, she spoke up, evidently disapproving of that last bit
of egotism, but all she murmured reprovingly, softly, was his
first name. Still, amazingly, it worked. He stopped in midtir-
ade, looked over at her, started to speak again, then shut up.
He got up from the couch and walked—stalked—to their
balcony.

I, thinking, *What the hell, the worst he can do is throw me
over,* followed him, which startled her into motion. She came
quickly behind me, her long skirts swishing over the marble
like ladies-in-waiting whispering behind my back.

"Dr. Lloyd?" When he turned his head slightly to acknowledge me, I advanced until I was leaning against the railing with
him. It was wrought iron, and I could only pray it was adequately bolted into the wall, all these stories up. But this wasn't
the time to show fear to him. At least he didn't have anything
in his hands that he could throw at me, as when he had hurled
a notebook at Carol. "I've been in situations like this before.
It's infuriating, I know it is, to donate your money with the
hope that it will go north and then to see it fly south instead.
I know that. You have my sympathy. You also have my word
that I will express your objections to the board of directors as
strongly as you have expressed them to me."

He looked at me then but with an intensity that made me
grip the railing even tighter. I hoped it didn't have a screw
loose, as he so clearly did. I didn't know what Dorothy Lloyd
was up to behind me, but the whispering ladies had stopped
talking.

"However, what I'm going to say is going to make you even
angrier. Here it is. You donated this money of your own free
will. You knew the terms. You took the chance. And you lost.
You bet on the wrong horse, Dr. Lloyd. I don't blame you if
you never give the Hart Foundation any more money, but this
money's gone. Legally. Even morally. You can fight it, you can
make everybody's life miserable, but in the end you'll still lose."

This was pure bluff on my part; maybe he didn't know that.

"And you want to know the underlying reason that you don't
have a chance?" I kept on even though I badly wanted to get
off that balcony and race to the elevator and back down to the

street, where I could be among comparatively sane folks—like the homeless mentally ill. "It's because you've chosen to back an organization that everybody but you seems to understand is a total scam. Dr. Lloyd, you ain't seen nothin' compared to what the Black Company has done to big money donors like you. They are scum, led by scum and fed by suckers. You want proof? I'll give you the phone numbers of ten, twenty, fifty black leaders I know, and they'll give you an earful—"

"*Liars!*" he screamed at me.

"*Now you just hold on!*" I raised my own voice against the wind of his fury, even though I knew better. Never argue with a drunk or a crazy person, that's my motto, which I forgot just when I needed to remember it. I was all set to scream right back at him, to defend the people I was speaking of, and to inform him, by God, that the Growth Fund garden he disdained was a hell of a lot worthier charity than the crooked one he so fanatically supported—I even had my index finger raised, preparatory to shaking it in his face—when his wife plucked me off the balcony.

Thank goodness somebody showed some sense!

He followed us into the living room, where she picked up my briefcase for me, shoved it at me, and tugged me over to the elevator where she pushed the button repeatedly until it appeared. Her husband was coming toward us like a bull charging just as the elevator doors closed on me.

When I approached the doorman, he held out a phone to me.

"Hello?" I said cautiously.

"Please, forgive my husband," said the soft, accented voice on the other end. "I'll talk to him, I'll try to calm him, but I must tell you, as I told Carol Margolis, poor child, that you may expect only problems from this decision of your board of directors. They shouldn't have done this to us, and they know perfectly well why that is."

"Please, Mrs. Lloyd, tell me why."

"Because the founder of the Black Company is my husband's brother, of course."

"Oh, lord, well then why didn't you just give the money to him?"

"They don't speak, haven't for years. My brother-in-law won't take any help or advice from Malcolm. So channeling our funds through a foundation was one way to do the same thing without his knowing. And now you've defeated us, and that money's gone."

"I haven't—"

"No good will come of this." She sounded desperately upset; her voice had dropped to a whisper. "It frightens me."

"What does, Mrs. Lloyd?"

"He's so very angry. I don't know what to do."

Abruptly, she hung up.

"Move out," I murmured as I handed the receiver back to the doorman. *And change your name and get an unlisted number. Maybe go into the FBI relocation program, get plastic surgery to change your face. But get away from that man!* He might be mad at us, but she was the one within hitting range.

"The man's nuts," I said to the doorman.

"A fuckin' praline," he agreed.

He ushered me out the front doors.

I walked into a cool, bright New York City night.

19

M Y INTENTION WAS TO HAIL A CAB TO TAKE ME HOME. BUT although Central Park South was thick with yellow taxis, none of them had their on-duty sign lighted to show they were available. Their passengers all looked New York elegant to me as they whizzed by on this blue, starry night in front of the most famous park in the world. I imagined they were going to the theater. Or they were on their way to dine. Or maybe they were traveling crosstown after late sessions at their shrinks' offices, and now they were heading to cocktail parties on Central Park West. Their lives looked glittery; they appeared like characters from an F. Scott Fitzgerald short story (with the fashions updated a bit) creatures from a planet where everybody lived on caviar and champagne. There were nearly as many limousines—great black mysterious cars and vast white stretch jobs that made me smile to see them because they looked so absurd, like a joke premise for an old-time movie: *Hey, guys, let's take a car and see how long we can stretch it, that'll really bring down the house!*

Down Fifty-ninth Street to my right was the Plaza Hotel and to my left, the St. Moritz Hotel. Beyond that was Columbus Circle, and if you walked straight north from there, you'd stroll the western edge of the park, up toward the Spooky Dakota, where ghosts and famous people lived, on to the Museum of Natural History, and further, further, further north was the high school where I'd felt like an alien this afternoon. That was another planet, too, where people didn't leave their shrinks' offices for evenings at the theater and where the glitter was broken glass. Behind me, to the south and east, lay Brooklyn, the quiet planet where Evelyn and Marty grieved their lost daughter and plotted the downfall of their hated son-in-law and Mrs. Marguerite Stewart and her son Robin ran their bed and breakfast for felons.

Central Park lay right across from where I was standing. There were horses and carriages lined up at the curb in front of it, waiting their turns to ferry tourists around the block or further. A ripe smell of horseflesh, hay, and manure wafted from their direction. The dark park was another planet altogether, where things were happening right now, the moment I stood gazing at it, in its interior and on its fringes, innocent things, malicious things, romantic things, haunting things, peaceful things, frightening things. Nobody sane or honest walked the park at dark, I figured, but it looked to me as if half of Manhattan was walking the borders of the park tonight.

"Must be all the people who couldn't catch a cab," I muttered.

Like me at that moment.

The subway was out of the question; that left walking.

I'd always heard it was safe to walk in midtown Manhattan at night, safer than in many smaller cities, because here there was so much light, so much activity, so much commerce in the shops and restaurants. Starkly opposed to that theory was the fact of Carol's death. But people did claim that usually there were just so many people on the streets of midtown after dark that you could feel safe, even if you weren't quite. I considered: I had to travel only about twenty blocks uptown and a few blocks west to Carol's place, a mere leisurely stroll to your average New Yorker.

I decided I'd walk it, at least as far as the lights and the traffic held out, and then if I had to, I could slip into a restaurant to call a cab.

I set out afoot into the bustle of New York City at night.

It was not a stupid thing to do, I told myself.

I'd always heard it was safe.

You're such a tourist! mocked Steve Wolff's voice in my head.
*You practically hyperventilate if you have to cross the street by
yourself!*

When I drew near to Carol's building an hour later, I was
still whole in mind and body, having been totally nonaccosted
by anybody along my route. I felt vindicated and justified. Not
to mention foolish. It *had* been safe. I hadn't been stupid. I
hadn't been robbed, mugged, beaten, raped, or killed. And I'd
gotten plenty of exercise, pushing along at my adrenaline-
rushed pace. Next time, I'd meander at a more sophisticated
pace, with the easy assurance of a native New Yorker, now that
I knew it was safe . . .

Turning the corner onto Riverside, I looked north and saw
an ambulance, its lights quietly throbbing, in the street in front
of Carol's building.

I picked up my pace.

Jed was there, peering into the rear window of the vehicle.
A driver was sliding quickly behind the steering wheel, and a
second paramedic was closing the passenger side door.

It pulled away before I got there.

Its siren started with a couple of jerks of sound, and then its
steady shriek invaded the quiet street until it seemed to thread
into every window, past every door, into every startled ear that
heard it.

"Who's in there, Jed?"

He looked at me strangely, as if he wasn't really seeing me.
"Mrs. Amory. Remember her? The jumper in 2C."

"Oh, my God, she finally did it?"

"Yeah." He stared up to where her apartment window was,
the one she'd straddled when he'd pulled her off the ledge just
the day before. "She got by me this time. Pretty poor service,
huh? Usually, we give great service around here. Carry your
bags, call your doctor. Screw in your lightbulbs, haul you off
windowsills. That's me, Superdoorman. Superfuckup this time."

"Jed, it couldn't be your fault."

"I was halfway to the window to get her."

"Oh, Jed, I'm so sorry—"

Suddenly, he grinned maniacally. "Oops!"

He loped off, back into the building and his own apartment,

leaving me blinking on the sidewalk. I stared up at the window from which the old lady had jumped or fallen and could have sworn I saw the death membrane, ripped right up the middle, its gossamer edges fluttering in the breeze.

When I climbed the five floors to my lodgings, I felt as tired as if I had personally lived all thirteen million lives in the naked city that day. There was an angel food cake, dribbled with pink icing, in a covered plastic dish, in front of my door.

"If it makes you happy, Mrs. Golding," I muttered.

I called my husband and left a message on our answering machine, telling him to expect Jed to let him in tomorrow night.

"I'm going to bed," I told him through the machine. "Don't call me."

I hung up without remembering to say, "I love you."

Upon pulling a nightgown out of the drawer I was using for lingerie, I saw that the tissue in which my new lovelies had been wrapped was disturbed. I pulled it back, then frantically, nearly weeping, rummaging through the drawer, then through all of the other drawers. I couldn't believe it! This apartment of Carol's was Grand Fucking Central Station! People walking in and out, leaving baskets of food, taking brand new underwear! Give me a break!

"Somebody's stolen my underwear, Carol!" I wailed. "What kind of place do you live in anyway! This just frosts it! This just really frosts it!"

I pulled out the bed, I slammed my head into the pillows, and I went to sleep.

I woke up in the middle of the night thinking about Carol. Didn't want to. It horrified me. Couldn't stop.

I lay there unable to stop thinking about her.

I kept "seeing" her running the night she died, in the few minutes before it happened. *Oh, Carol. Take another route, turn left instead of right, run different streets, don't even go out at all that night. Stay home, get sick, don't go out!* I wanted to reach through time to snatch her out of danger and toss her back into her apartment, make her sprain her ankle so she couldn't run, erase her separation from Steve, so she'd still be running in the mornings. What was she thinking as she ran toward her death? I imagined it, the sorts of ordinary thoughts she might have had, about work, about the divorce, about her parents, about her "problem," and about the person who would hate her if she solved it. Did she have a premonition as she stopped to drink her coffee at the Cafe O'Lay or maybe in the few seconds before she ran straight into death?

Did she recognize him . . . death?

I "saw" another runner, coming up behind her, calling her name, stopping her, moving in close to her. It was a man in a jogging suit with a hood covering his scalp and the sides of his face, so that she could see him, but nobody else could make out his features. Was he black, white? Tall, short? Fat, thin? The faces of the people I'd met flitted across the countenance of the phantom . . . Had I met her killer?

Pretty soon, I had myself scared sleepless.

And then the tears started to flow again.

"And," I sniffed before I dozed off, "how about the creep who stole my underwear?"

20

T HE SECOND TIME I WOKE UP, IT WAS TWO HOURS LATER, and the phone was ringing. I grabbed it blindly.

"Patty Vinitsky, Jenny."

I yawned. "What time is it?"

"Seven-thirty. Wake up, we have a problem. Get down to the garden as soon as you can—"

"Garden?" My brain hadn't kicked in yet. She wanted me to garden at seven-thirty in the morning? This was a dream, that's what it was, and if I gently hung up the telephone, she would go away—

"Come on, wake up. Growth Fund. The Lloyds, Dorothy and Malcolm."

"Oh, right, I saw them last night. The garden." Suddenly, I was awake. "What problem?"

"It's the Garden of Evil this morning. He got in there last night, Dr. Lloyd did, and he destroyed it."

"I don't understand."

"Tore, ripped, shredded, he dug it up, literally plowed up nearly every square inch of that garden. They are up . . . set. Oh, my, are they upset. The police are upset. They are looking for him, everybody's looking for him. They are looking for us, for any of us, me, you. And it's got to be you, because I have an appearance in court this morning, and trust me, none of the other directors is up to this level of crisis. I know you don't know these people—"

"Never met them—"

"I know, I know, but you have to handle it. Go over there. Offer them something, anything, Jesus, tell them our entire board will plant roses for them, I don't care. Just don't let them sue us, and try to keep them from lynching Dr. Lloyd. They think he's ours. Hell, he is ours. You want to know what that son of a bitch did to us, Jenny?"

"Tell me the worst."

"He left a sign that said Hartbreak. Spelled h-a-r-t. Clever bastard, isn't he? Don't let them kill him. Don't let the cops take him."

"How can I stop that? I'm no attorney, you're the—"

"I want to kill him. Save him for me. He is mine. And by the way, now that I have you on the line, two more things, no three: What the hell did you say to Andrei Bolen yesterday? He called me, all upset. I told him not to worry, you'd soon have a recommendation for me to give the board. Right?" She didn't give me time to argue but tore right into numbers two and three. "Two, Damon Calendar's on my back again, says why didn't you show up for your appointment at the theater with him yesterday—"

"Why, that—"

"I know, I know. Try again today. And Mrs. Stewart's son, Robin, called to invite you to dinner out there tonight. I thought you said she didn't like you?"

"I thought she didn't. What time did he say?"

"Eightish. I can't be taking all these messages for you, Jenny."

"I'll turn on the answering machine."

I realized only then that I hadn't done that, an omission that seemed blatantly Freudian, even to me. Afraid of getting any more messages, was I? Or was it simply that it meant I'd have to erase her voice and substitute my own.

"Pat, how do they know for sure it was Dr. Lloyd who did it?"

The laugh that came over the line was sepulchral, and it was a bitter ghost who laughed it. "He was seen. People reported seeing a burly black man getting into a Mercedes. I gather this was only *after* he hacked the damned wisteria down."

"But that could have been any—"

"Wearing surgical greens."

"Oh, shit, and wielding a scalpel, no doubt."

"Probably."

There was a certain cosmic and appropriately black humor about all this, but I managed to keep my cosmic black amusement out of my voice as I promised to hie myself over to the garden and said good-bye to her. "Good thing I've got those baked goods of Ida's," I said to myself, "or I'd miss breakfast." In ten minutes, I was down the stairs and running hard for the first available intersection where I could catch a crosstown bus or an uptown cab. A cab got there first. I ate an entire miniature loaf of zucchini bread on the way and told the cabbie I had to have a cup of coffee or die. He screeched to a stop in front of the Cafe O'Lay so that I could run in, order and pay for two cappuccinos to go, and return to his back seat almost before his meter turned over. My doorman, Jed, walked in as I walked out, and we greeted each other hurriedly. I wondered if he'd slept any better than I had; all things considered, probably not. Steve Wolff was right, I reflected, as I lifted the lid on the first cup of coffee: This was just a small town, where everybody knew everybody else. By the time my taxi reached the garden, I was hot steppin' it on sugar and caffeine.

"Lookit, willya?" the cabbie demanded when we got our first glimpse of the garden block. There were two police cars at the curb and there were grown men and women running about and looking hysterical inside the high fence. "Whatdaya think happened here? A mass murder?"

"Sumpin' like that," I agreed grimly.

It was a mass murder and not only of defenseless baby vegetables and flowers.

"He killed our dreams," a black woman said, oblivious to my approach. She was seated on the ground, sifting earth through her shaking fingers and weeping over it. "Hours," she moaned to herself. "So many hours, so many hopes, and he's killed all of them." When she did glance up at me, I saw utter hatred in her eyes. "I hate him. I hope somebody plants a stake in his heart and he rots and composts and they grow tomatoes out of him."

"But there was a guard!" I·protested.

Her eyes were overflowing with tears. "He tricked our man. He said it was him who paid for this garden. He said he wanted to take a turn guarding it. He said our man could go on home, that he'd take care of things till the next shift."

Diabolical, I thought. Incredibly, cleverly wicked.

"What was our man supposed to say?" she cried.

"Anybody would have left then," I agreed. "I'd have believed him."

She grabbed a clump of dirt and hurled it blindly away from her. "I hate him, a doctor, can you believe that a doctor would do something like this? I can't believe it! I could kill him."

I patted her back and then went looking for somebody in charge.

All about me was devastation. Wooden stakes and arbors that looked as if they had been lovingly sawed in somebody's basement lay broken. The little red ribbons that had been tied to those stakes were smashed forlornly into the ground. Newly sprouting plants—it was early spring yet—had been rousted violently from their warm, wet incubator of earth, and now their delicate little root systems lay trampled under our feet. Clay flower pots were reduced to shards, and the tin tool shed was battered as if by a sledgehammer, as if it had been through a hail storm with hail the size of fists. But the worst of the ruin was visible in the heartbroken faces of the local gardeners. I saw tears, I saw naked fury, I saw incredible pain and discouragement written on those black, white, brown, and golden faces. There were children on hand who wore the look of those children captured in war photographs for *Time* or *Newsweek*. Their little faces seemed to ask, *This is life? This is how adults are?*

I grabbed the first cop I saw and introduced myself.

"I represent the Hart Foundation, which funds this garden."

"You got insurance for these people?"

"I don't know. Is there anything else I can do to help?"

"Yeah, you can find us the fucking asshole lunatic who did

this to this beautiful garden. Who would do this to these people? First ray of hope they've seen in some of their lifetimes.
This was going to help feed a bunch of families this year, you
know that? Vegetables to take home with them and a whole lot
to sell. Compost, they were making compost to sell as fertilizer
to suburbanites, you know? Good work they were doing, it was
a real boon to their neighborhood, makin' people feel good,
just to look at it, even the punks, the kids. Now and then they
even helped. Hell, now and then I even helped. I loved this
garden. Everybody loved it." He snorted. "Well, obviously not
everybody. One fucking asshole had a grudge." He eyed me
with disfavor. "I understand he was pissed at you folks, that's
why he did this."

"Who are we talking about?"

"Doctor Malcolm "Green Thumb" Lloyd, that's who, and you
know it. Chop off his thumbs, that's what they ought to do,
and I'd stand by and watch them do it, too. Might even hand
them the scalpel. See how he likes that, him and his surgery
on these people and their garden. Amputated it, he did. Sev-
ered an artery in this neighborhood, a life-giving artery, was
going to revive them, bring some of them back to life, and he
fucking slipped his knife in and cut it, and now they're bleed-
ing. Oh, it hurts, this does. It hurts these people, hurts us to
know what's going to come as a result of it. Good thing the
man's black, that's all I can say, and we'll be lucky there ain't
some fighting going on anyway. What'd you do to tick him off,
what'd you people do to make anybody mad enough to do this
much damage?"

"We donated his money to this garden."

That briefly stopped his tirade. It was difficult for him to
pinpoint the bad guy in that scenario. "Okay, well, you want
to help them now? Then tell me where to find the doctor."

"You probably know his address, and other than that, I can't
help you. I only met the man myself last night. I'm so new on
the job I've never even been in this garden before."

"Well, you're a big help, aren't you?"

"Listen, this is awful, and I'm sorry about it."

"Okay," he conceded. "Yeah, me, too."

He directed me to a young black couple standing by the

remains of the tool shed. I approached them gingerly, expecting a blast like the one the cop had leveled at me.

"Excuse me?"

As one, they turned toward me, like book pages opening and, lordy, they were smiling. Not big smiles, granted, but nice ones. I didn't expect those smiles to linger when I introduced myself and my purpose.

"I'm Jenny Cain. I'm taking Carol Margolis's place at the Hart Foundation—"

Sure enough, frowns descended, but it turned out to be for a different reason than I anticipated. The woman spoke first. "Oh, I'm so sorry about poor Carol. She was a dear, so wonderful to us. The only blessing is that she can't see what that awful man has done to us. She'd have a fit, I know, she'd be out here with the rest of us." This woman, however, seemed quite dry-eyed, markedly calmer than most of the other people around us. The good-looking young man beside her maintained a similar composure that seeped out of him—them—into me.

"I know," he said soothingly, so that I felt as if he'd laid a cool hand on my brow. "It's not your fault, it isn't anybody's fault, except for the person who committed this crime." He gazed around and even managed to laugh a little. "Now this is what you'd call a real 'crime against nature,' isn't it?"

They were the cochairs of the Growth Fund, it turned out. His name was Art and hers was Dell, short for Spidell, she said, and they told me they lived together, that it was the garden that had introduced them.

"I wish you could have seen this garden yesterday, Jenny," she said with a sigh. "So beautiful. So hopeful. Well," she said next, as if figuratively brushing old dirt off her hands and stepping forward toward a new chore, "if you want to know how you can help, how the foundation can help, that is—"

"Please, I do, we do. I think we'd do just about anything."

She looked me straight in the eyes and ticked off her requests: "Give us a check now so we can hire a bulldozer to come in and level this mess. We'll buy replacement seeds and starter plants and tools today. We'll put up another shed today. We'll have this garden replanted by the end of the weekend if you don't make us wait to untangle the insurance, if you give us the money to do it today." And Dell literally held out her palm to me, smiling a smile that said she didn't for a moment really believe I could do it.

And, in fact, I wasn't authorized to do any such thing. Nobody'd given me the Hart Foundation checkbook. So I did the only thing I could: Just as Dell smilingly started to withdraw her hand, I withdrew my own checkbook from my briefcase. People forget sometimes that I come from a wealthy family; hell, even I forget it sometimes, because Geof and I live fairly modestly, all things being relative. But it is there, a deep green pool of affluence from which I can pour drops or buckets into dry ponds if that's what I want to do with it.

"How much for this weekend's work?" I asked.

She blinked, started to grin, and didn't for a moment object.

"Let's say five hundred," she suggested, glancing for agreement at her friend, who shook his head in happy disbelief. Her smile grew mischievous, and she amended, "Oh, let's say six hundred, shall we?"

"No," I said, busy writing, "let's not."

She looked so surprised, as if I'd slapped her, that I quickly added, "What I mean is, let's say a thousand, and let's say you'll call me if this doesn't cover what you need until the foundation or the insurance comes through, all right?"

I handed a check to her.

She stared at it, then at me. "But this is your personal—"

"I'll be reimbursed."

Tears appeared in her eyes. I wasn't actually sure I would get the money back, but they didn't have to know that. She handed the check to Art, who impulsively grabbed me by my shoulders, pulled me into a bear hug, and kissed me. Then he left us, hurriedly loping off and calling out names of volunteers as he ran. They gathered around, and I saw him wave the check at them. In a moment, a ragged cheer broke out from the crowd surrounding him.

Spidell and I smiled at each other.

"How can you be so calm about this, Dell?"

She stubbed her right tennis shoe against a broken wooden stake and shrugged, looking up again with a gentle smile. "It's not people that died here. You see people dying all around you when you live in a place like I do, and it puts everything else in perspective. I can't raise those people from the dead, not my dad who died in jail, not my brother who died on the streets, and not my little sister who's dying right this minute from a crack habit. But I can resurrect this garden." Her smile glowed at me. "Thanks, Jenny."

I shrugged it off. "Easy."

"For you to say."

I laughed, and we impulsively hugged each other. "Don't be surprised," I said to her, "if some of our board members show up to dig in the dirt. And I'd suggest that if you ever wanted publicity for this project—"

"I already thought of that, we'll turn this into a blessing."

"If anybody can, it's you and Art."

"Easy," she said, shrugging.

"For you to say."

When I left to hail another cab, I turned and saw her wave at me. I waved back, and suddenly the lot was full of hands jauntily semaphoring at me. The chaos of despair was already being transformed by that young couple into the happy turmoil of strong purpose and renewed hope. Tears sprang to my own eyes this time, and by the time I squeezed into the back seat of yet another taxi, I was dabbing at my face with a tissue. "Thanks, Great-Grandpa," I whispered to the long-dead ancestor who'd made this moment possible. "How do you like this, all this way down through the generations, clear into a second century?"

My own cynicism cut the sentimentality as I thought: He'd have hated it! My male ancestors were all business, the Henry Fords of the clam-canning world, and from what I'd heard of them, they would never have given away a penny they could take to their graves. "Well, roll over," I advised them in those graves. "This is good for your souls."

And mine, I suspected.

"Central Park South," I directed the driver, like a native.

I intended to murder Dr. Malcolm Lloyd before anybody else got to him.

21

DOROTHY LLOYD WAS WAITING FOR ME WHEN THE ELEVA-
tor doors opened directly into her foyer.

"Do you know what he did?" I asked, stepping out.

"Yes, of course." She looked older, her face thinner, her
features more stark; she fiddled with the long African bead
necklace around her neck, twisting it nervously between her
fingers. "Police have been here. Police have called. Patricia
Vinitsky called. Now you. Of course, I know, of course."

As if compelled to movement, she walked onto the balcony.

"Don't ask the obvious," she commanded as I followed her.
"Don't ask me if he did it. Don't ask me where he is. Don't
ask me why. Yes, he did it, of course, he did. I don't know
where he is, and I haven't known since he stormed out of here
shortly after you left last night. As to why, you know why,
everyone knows why. Stop asking me!"

She clutched the railing and stared at the park far below us,
as if she might catch a glimpse of her husband darting between
the carriages.

"I don't think that explains it," I said.

"Of course, it does! In his own way, he is devoted to the
Black Company and to his brother."

"That may be an excuse, but it's no answer. Mrs. Lloyd,

141

maybe you haven't seen the garden, either before or after he destroyed it. Maybe you're not aware that most of the folks who created it and whom it will serve are black. It's a 'black company,' too. It will feed black families and bring them income. He devastated that, Mrs. Lloyd. Do you realize it is—was—as large as a city block? That's what he destroyed, a city block's worth of hope. Because he didn't like what we did with the money? That's a reason? Because he wanted to help his brother? That's a reason? No, no way. If this isn't pathological behavior, then I don't know what is. What's the next step in this escalation, Mrs. Lloyd? How much further does he have to go over the edge before he takes his scalpel and shoves it into somebody? And do you think you're safer than the rest of us? Do you think a man who's as far out of control as he is would hesitate to hurt anybody who got in his way, even you?"

She put her face in her hands and began to weep.

"My advice," I continued inexorably, because I truly believed her life might be at stake, "if the police haven't already suggested this, is for you to lock your doors and alert the doorman not to admit your husband. Better yet, leave this building altogether, without telling anybody where you're going. Go stay with friends he doesn't know. Check into a hotel where he wouldn't expect to find you. He will probably calm down for a while, he may try to come home, but please don't be alone here when he does. Make arrangements for him to be picked up by the police. Protect yourself and the other people in this building. And Mrs. Lloyd . . . just how angry was he at Carol Margolis?"

Through her weeping, she spoke in a terrible, lost voice. "I've been asking myself that question all morning."

I held out my hand and she grasped it like a lifeline.

"I really don't know," she whispered. "God help me."

As it turned out, I was the one who gave the orders to the doorman not to admit Dr. Lloyd if he showed up. But I left Central Park South not at all convinced that I had persuaded anybody of the danger, including his wife.

I called Pat Vinitsky from the nearest pay phone to report.

"You shouldn't have done that," she said of my personal financial bailout to the gardeners. "Sets a very bad precedent.

We can't just be handing people checks out of our personal accounts to cover them when they're short."

"I know that," I admitted. "I hope it doesn't cause you any problems. It seemed like the right thing to do at the time." Which was not the same as apologizing for it. (An objective part of my brain took note of how much I enjoyed acting autonomously, pretending I had no boss, nobody else to report to. And what did *that* mean I wanted to be when I grew up?)

"Now," she said, "you can go back and write a positive Book'Em evaluation report for me to take to the board."

I took a deep breath and attempted to clear the Lloyd fiasco from the front of my mind. "I'm not feeling very positive about it, Pat."

There was a short silence, and then she exploded. "Don't tell me that, Jenny, I don't want to hear it. I don't give a damn how you feel about it. I'm telling you it's a fabulous project that the foundation wants to fund. I don't need any negative crap from you about it. I got enough of that from Carol. You just get that report in and forget your personal opinions about it. I've got all the opinions we need on this subject, and mine are totally positive. I've never seen a project I supported as much as I do this one. That school needs it. This city needs it. And Andrei needs it. Don't you go all tight-assed on me, Jenny, you don't know anything about this city or our schools or our kids. We'll decide what we need. You just fill in the forms and hand them in to me. This afternoon. Got it? This is not a permanent job, remember, and it can be a hell of a lot more temporary than it already is."

"That's pretty weak blackmail, Pat."

"Don't be absurd. I'm only stating facts."

"No, you're telling me that if I don't twist my opinions to fit your version of the facts, you'll dump me. That's a wonderfully attractive threat after the morning I've had. Do make good on it, Pat. I'd be grateful, why I'd be so grateful that I'd take the first plane out of here."

"Now wait, I didn't mean—"

"You can close up the apartment for me. You can get on the phone and locate another interim director. You can have dinner tonight with the Stewarts. You can deal with Damon Calendar at the theater. You can handle the Lloyd situation." I laughed a little. "And, best of all, you can deal with . . . you."

There was another silence as her devious little lawyer's mind worked double time to try to find a way around those unopposable arguments. When she caved in, it was so sweet I nearly tasted sugar on my tongue. She forced a laugh to make me think it was all a bluff, all in a day's work of negotiating terms.

"Give the project one more look, will you? Just a fair shake before you write your report, is that too much to ask?"

"Of course not." I was insultingly magnanimous. My voice took on a full, warm, rich, obnoxious tone of forbearance, like a balloon overstuffed with hot air. "I'll be happy to do that."

"Good for you," she said dryly.

I laughed, I couldn't help it.

Pat Vinitsky laughed, too, though it had an edge to it.

I couldn't wait to get off the phone, and I felt relieved when it finally happened. Looking around me at the New Yorkers rushing here and there, I thought; *What is it with you guys, since I got here? Is the moon full? Is it in the water? Is this the way it always is?* A horrifying thought. How could anybody live constantly on the edge like this? On the other hand, it certainly kept me revved up. And since I was—revved up, that is—I decided to stage another foray into the Village to see if I could get into the theater to meet Damon Calendar, to whom I planned to present a piece of my mind. The nerve of the man, complaining to Vinitsky that *I* had missed our appointment!

22

I T WAS ANOTHER WASTED TRIP.

The doors were still locked, and my knocking and yelling didn't generate any more response than it had the day before. The posters advertising the play were still in place, however, and still offering the news that the opening would be tomorrow night. I wrote down the number to call for tickets: If they wouldn't let me in today, I'd pay my way in tomorrow night. I only hoped that Geof liked *King Lear*.

"I knew this would happen," I muttered as I turned away.

Having admitted that, I then had to confess my real motive for the trip back down there, which was to buy replacement lingerie for my reunion with my husband that night. I argued with myself briefly, excuse the pun, over the extra expense, and I could almost hear Geof tell me not to bother, as I wouldn't be wearing them long enough to make a difference anyway. That delicious thought distracted me so that I nearly walked into a post. But I also loved the thought of how he'd melt when he saw them.

"Whoo," I said, fanning myself with my hand. "Down, girl."

And I thought I could survive without him for whole weeks at a time as a commuter wife?

"Buy the drawers, kiddo, and get back to work."

The second set wasn't as pretty as the first or quite as sexy, which made me feel angry and disappointed all over again. I wanted to complain to somebody, preferably to Carol. Upon checking my watch, I discovered that it was almost lunch hour, and I decided that I deserved a nice, long one. I knew just who I wanted to spend it with, too: Jed's mother.

"*Who is it?*" a woman's voice demanded from inside the apartment at the rear of the lobby. "*What is it?*"

"Jenny Cain. From Carol's apartment. I want to see you."

"Oh, hell, wait a minute." It took about that long for her to loosen her many locks and then for her to snatch her door open and to reveal herself standing there in all her glory. And a glory she was in a purple velvet dressing gown with purple silk mules on her feet and her hair piled high behind a massive purple bow on her head. Her mouth was a Clara Bow Kewpie doll's, and her cheeks and the end of her nose were perfectly painted circles of pink. I couldn't take my eyes off the faint pink at the tip of her nose. She looked as if a clown had kissed her three times. And all of that wasn't even the odd part: The weird thing about it was that this was not an old woman dressed up in this dated frippery; no, she looked only about fifteen years older than her son, which made her all of about thirty-four, younger than I was, by just a hair, of course.

"What do you want?" she demanded again. "I don't mean to be rude, but everybody here knows this is my time to watch my old timey movies, and it's a Marlene Dietrich this afternoon and I'm right in the middle of it, and I hate to miss it."

Gesturing toward her outfit, I said, "Is that why . . . do you dress up to . . . ?"

"Yeah." She slung one arm up along the side of the open door as casually as if she were wearing blue jeans and a sweatshirt. "I like to play dress up, always have, ever since I was a girl. Should have been a fashion model, everybody says I was pretty enough, but I'm too short, should have been tall like you."

I heard Jimmy Stewart's voice coming from a television.

"*Witness for the Prosecution?*" I guessed.

"Yeah." She waved her free hand as if she were splashing water with it, a hurry-up signal to me. "So, what is it?"

"Well, first of all, I nearly killed myself the other night on the stairs because your tenant in 5C had turned all the hall lights off."

"No, he didn't."

I stared at her. "Yes! He did."

"Who says?"

"Mrs. Golding told me that he does it all the—"

Jed's mother laughed and made a derogatory motion with her hand as if to say, *Oh, her!*

"Have you spoken to him about it?"

"Why should I speak to him about it?"

I was getting nowhere. So I tried the next topic. "Okay, then let me ask you this . . . Who has access to Carol's apartment?"

"Why?"

"Something was stolen from it yesterday."

"Nah, you just lost it."

"No! I put it in a drawer."

"What was it?"

"New clothes."

She eyed my own outfit critically as if to say, *Steal your clothes? God, who'd want to?*

"Underwear," I added with wounded dignity.

Her attention was momentarily distracted by Dietrich's voice. "Shit! My favorite part's coming up. So what'd you ask me?"

"Who could have gotten into my room yesterday?"

"Me, I go up there every day to make sure you got the toilet turned off, that one tends to stick, drives the old lady below you crazy, so I check it. Jed could have if you had a delivery or something. I think Mrs. Golding has a key, because Carol gave her one. Her husband, I suppose he still has his. I don't know who else. Oh, she's on the witness stand! I have to go see this, you got to excuse me!"

And she closed the door in my face.

I didn't even get a chance to ask her how Mrs. Amory was doing and what was it a son could do that even a mother couldn't forgive? What an impossible woman! She'd deny the sun came up if it was shining in her face! Out of sheer pique, I was half-inclined to think she was probably the one who stole my stuff; a little Victorian dressup might have appealed to her sense of costume adventure. For all I knew, she was wearing it now, under that awful purple dressing gown. Truth to the tell, I was still feeling a bit stung by her silent commentary on *my* fashion sense.

Was it *that* conservative?

I spent the rest of the afternoon in Carol's office catching up on routine business for the Hart Foundation. Before I dressed for my dinner in Brooklyn with the unpredictable Stewarts, mother and son, I placed a late afternoon call to Mrs. Dorothy Lloyd.

"Have you heard from your husband, Mrs. Lloyd?"

"No," she claimed, "not yet."

"I still wish you'd get away from there."

"I'm thinking about it," was all she would concede.

By the time she made up her mind, I thought after I hung up, that lovely woman could be beaten or dead. But in thinking that, I—like Dr. Malcolm Lloyd—bet on the wrong horse.

Robin Stewart was all genial smiles when he greeted me at the front door, but his first words were dismaying.

"I'll apologize before I even say hello, Jenny. Mother's changed her mind again, she's not coming down to dinner after all." His overgrown shock of white hair hung boyishly over his eyes as he held open the screen door for me. From the street, the spooky old mansion in Brooklyn had looked downright festive, with lights pouring from its windows. Inside, there was a hum of voices, all tenor and bass, which sounded cheerful until you gave careful thought to its source. Then it took on the air of a penitentiary just before the prisoners moved from their cells into the cafeteria. I stepped into the foyer and handed him my coat as he said, "You must think we're awful, jerking you back and forth like this, but I can't say I'm sorry about *that*, because *I'm* glad you're here. I'll try to make it all up to you with a decent dinner and good company." He got a funny

148

smile on his lined, pale face. "Well, unique company at least. I can pretty well guarantee you'll never have another dinner quite like this."

"Why'd she change her mind, Robin?"

He put out his left hand but didn't actually touch me, as he ushered me into the dining room. I'd expected to see the long table set for three, with places for him, his mother, and me, but every place was set.

"Oh, who knows?"

I stopped him as he began to pull out a chair for me. Apparently, I was to sit at the table in regal solitude while I waited for everyone else to appear.

"Robin, you don't have to do this, maybe I should leave—"

"No! It's a treat to have another woman in the house. I've seen enough of men to last me a lifetime. No, stay, please."

I sat down in the chair he proffered to me.

He disappeared through swinging doors into the kitchen and soon the table began to fill up with food brought in by several different men, and within minutes after that, there were nine men and me gathered around the big table, digging into huge platters of spaghetti and long loaves of hot garlic bread. Robin took a seat at the head of the table, like Dad, and I was ensconced at the opposite end, like Mom. Or maybe we were Robin Hood and Maid Marian. He quickly introduced me to Fred the counterfeiter, Robinson the sex offender, Paulie the arsonist, Eddie the enforcer, Manny the armed robber, and three murderers: Jackson, Quillin, and Allen Cheskey, the one who'd showed me to Mrs. Stewart's room on the day before.

It was unnerving but weirdly entertaining—if you could manage not to think about details like innocent victims—because they regaled me with stories of their crimes and incarcerations as if they were characters in a crime caper novel by Randy Russell or Donald Westlake. To hear them tell it, they were all smarter than everybody else, just unluckier. If there was a particle of repentance among them, I didn't hear it.

A couple of them didn't partake in the frivolity. Allen Cheskey appeared bored by it all and was the first to finish and take his plate to the kitchen.

"Our little dishwasher," one of the men snickered quietly.

"He washes dishes in a cafe," another of them explained to me.

Robinson the sex offender stared at me all through dinner without saying a word. Whenever I noticed him, however, I wanted to utter five words: Get me out of here.

Eventually, with a great show of gruff masculine courtesy, the other residents of the Stewart ménage took their leave of Robin and me.

"Bowling night," he explained.

I couldn't help but laugh.

"I know." He laughed, too. "It's some team, isn't it? Murderers and rapists and thieves? Some of them don't roll the ball down the lane so much as they throw it down like they're going to kill the pins. And you have to watch them like crazy or some of them will cheat on the scores, and then you may have a fight on your hands. They're not supposed to drink on these nights—they're not supposed to use alcohol at all—but they sneak beers and then it's testosterone city in the house for hours. Keeps her awake." He rolled his gaze toward the ceiling. "Then Cheskey has to sit up with her till all hours to keep her happy."

"He's a favorite of hers?"

"He's her lapdog." Robin smiled in a self-satisfied way as he leaned back in his chair and laced his fingers over his stomach. "I don't know what I'd do without my favorite little murderer. Allen's been here for years, and I hope he stays until the day she kicks off. He takes care of her, which relieves me of the necessity. Waits on her hand and foot. Spoils her, of course, but at least he keeps her out of my hair." His expression was deeply cynical. "Everybody ought to have an Allen of their very own. Pathologically devoted, fanatically hardworking, loyal as a dog, and, at heart, mean as a pit bull. Get yourself one, Jenny. They're a dime a dozen down at the human pound."

"Prison?"

He nodded and laughed.

"May I see your mother, Robin?"

He looked startled. "Why?"

"I'd like to make one last try."

But he shook his head. "No, because I don't want her upset, not with Allen gone. Sometimes I can handle her, like yesterday, but even then he had to go up and hold her hand, calm her down. Anyway, it wouldn't do any good; she's so unpredictable."

"Oh, I don't know," I muttered under my breath. An idea was forming in my head, and I wished so much that I could check it out with Carol to see if she'd confirm it.

"What?"

"Nothing. I've got to be getting back."

He looked disappointed. "Really? I was hoping you could stay and keep me company. We could watch a movie or something." Was there the suggestion of a leer in his eyes now? "Everybody's gone."

I suppressed the shudder I felt.

"Sorry, my husband's coming into town tonight."

"You're married?" He glanced down at my left hand, where I wasn't wearing a ring, because I never did, and Geof didn't either. Another idea was forming in my head, which was that Mrs. Stewart hadn't had anything to do with this invitation to dinner and that she probably didn't even know I was here. "Oh. Well. Ice cream?"

I tactfully declined dessert.

Robin abruptly pushed back from the table. Obviously, I'd dashed his hopes. "I have to take a plate of spaghetti up to her. You can wait here if you want to or take a look around the house. This won't take long, but I'll probably have to hang around and talk to her for a few minutes."

He sighed in a put-upon manner and left the dining room.

While he put together a tray for his mother, I remained seated at the table, rapidly pondering the implications of charitable remainder trusts. About the time I heard him go out another kitchen door, I began to feel sure enough of my theory to risk propounding it to somebody else.

I listened for his footsteps on the stairs.

When I heard him on the landing above, I walked quickly into the foyer to get my trench coat and put it on, so that it might appear that I had already left the house. Then I waited around the corner until Robin came down. When he disappeared into the kitchen again, I quietly climbed the carpeted stairs to the second floor. I heard his voice downstairs say, "Jenny, you still here?" just as I approached the French doors that opened onto his mother's bedroom.

*   *   *

She was still planted in her luxurious, messy bed, still clothed in the pink bedjacket, still watching the television, and now slurping long strands of pasta into her mouth.

The TV was so loud she didn't hear me come in.

That was fine, as it allowed me to walk closer to her—before she could stop me—so that I could talk to her without yelling. I didn't want Robin to overhear what I had to ask her; that wouldn't have been fair, not even to him. It wasn't my business to drive a final wedge between mother and son; my only business was the Hart foundation and Carol.

"Mrs. Stewart," I said, "I have a message for you."

She nearly spilled her tray of food, and I had to reach out my hands to help her steady it. I was afraid that any minute she'd start bleating for help again to try to ward me off—me and the unpleasant truth.

"I'll just say it and get out of here."

She waited, wary as a cornered badger.

"I discovered a memo that Carol Margolis wrote that she never intended anyone else to see." This was a total fabrication, of course. If only Carol had left such a memorandum! I wouldn't have such a feeling of standing on a high dive and plunging off into a pool that might not have any water in it. The old badger in the bed was looking increasingly agitated, but I suspected that now she would listen to me and that she wouldn't dare to call to her son for help. "The memo explains how you asked her to set up a charitable remainder trust with the Hart Foundation so that it would appear that when you died, all of the income from the trust would go to your son for the rest of his life and then when he died, it would all devolve to the foundation."

She was looking at me with hatred, dread, anticipation.

"But the memo also says that it was all a lie. You only want your son to *think* he's getting the money, so that you can keep him under control during your lifetime. The truth is, you don't plan to leave any money to him, do you? You've never given him anything during your lifetime, and you don't intend to change that when you die. You think he'll close this halfway house, spend all your money, waste it. But Carol wouldn't go along with the lie, even though it meant a lot of money for the foundation."

I waited for her to deny it, any part of it.

She shifted her gaze from me back to the television and started eating her spaghetti again, though I saw that the hand that lifted the fork was trembling, but not with fear or shame, I thought, merely with anger.

After another thirty seconds, I walked out.

Robin was standing outside the French doors.

"Who's she leaving it to?"

His voice was tight, his face looked shocked.

"It might not even be true, Robin."

But I suspected I knew and that he'd eventually figure it out, too. Who was it who really cared for his mother, who was fanatically devoted to her, even pathologically loyal, according to his own description? I didn't want to answer any more of his questions or to stay in that house any longer than I had to, and so I brushed past him and went quickly down the stairs and out the front door, without even pausing to call for a taxi to take me back into Manhattan.

23

I HURRIED AWAY FROM THAT STRANGE MANSION WHERE A MAN who hated his mother ran a halfway house for other men who'd killed, raped, robbed, and beaten.

It was only when I found myself on Flatbush Avenue that I realized I hadn't seen a taxi since I left the Stewarts'. I glanced at my watch. Damn. It was very late, Geof might even be in by now, and he'd probably be worrying about little ol' me, off by myself in the big, bad city. I looked around and suddenly began to feel some of his trepidations creep into my own mind: It was very dark, even with the streetlights, the stores were closed, there wasn't much traffic, and the pedestrians didn't all look like folks you'd want to trust to hold your purse while you bent down to tie your shoelaces.

How was I going to get home?

"Eh, baby," whispered a young man who slid past me like grease oozing out of a sandwich. "Wanta play, sweetheart?"

Suddenly, the subway looked inviting, or if not exactly inviting, at least like the only remaining alternative. I ran underground. Unfamiliar with the routine of taking the train, I wasted minutes attempting to decipher the subway map until I finally figured out which trains to take and where to transfer to get through Brooklyn, under the river, and across town again to the Upper West Side. Then I fumbled my way through the turnstile, trotted up to the track, and passionately wished there were a lot more people around than there were. I had to wait an agonizing twenty minutes and watch two wrong trains go by—all the while also watching my own violent fantasies play in my head—before the right train screeched to a stop in front of me.

I boarded and took a seat on a two-person bench in the nearly empty car.

The train started up again.

Though I leaned back, I couldn't relax. I still had to get to the other end of the city without getting mugged. All my worst fears about New York subways, every horrible fate I'd ever heard, got on that train and rode along with me.

I turned my face to the dirty window, staring at the dark, blank walls clacking by. The next station came quickly, and the train slowed to a halt, took on passengers, and then racketed on to the next stop.

"Excuse me."

A heavy person sank down on the bench next to me.

I turned to look.

"Hello," said Allen Cheskey. His tanned, bald scalp gleamed under the lights in the train and the small diamond earring in his right ear winked at me. His strong-featured face was as expressionless as always, but his words were full of meaning.

"Mrs. Stewart says you don't want to say anything to anybody."

I cleared my throat and merely stared at him.

"She says that would be best. I think so, too."

After a moment, when I thought my voice would work, I said, "I thought you went bowling."

"And leave her alone? No way. I stick around."

Did you "stick" Carol? I wanted to ask. Did you threaten her, or did you just go ahead and make sure she couldn't tell anybody what your mistress had planned for her son and for you? I surmised that what Mrs. Stewart wanted to do wasn't illegal, but it was certainly immoral, and if Carol had blabbed, Mrs. Stewart would have lost control of her son for all time.

"What will happen if I do tell somebody?"

He turned his mirrorlike stare on me again and shrugged, a

most chilling gesture coming from him. "We'll sue you for slander, you and that foundation. Make it expensive for you, give you a lot of bad publicity. It's your word against hers, there's nothing written down, nothing you can prove."

It seemed an oddly toothless threat, considering what I expected.

And he seemed to have forgotten the "memo" I'd "found." Maybe they didn't believe that; maybe it was sufficient to know I'd detected the truth about their lie.

I wanted to get away from him. I didn't want him to follow me all the way into Manhattan or to know so easily where I lived. The signs whizzing by told me our next stop was Brooklyn Heights, and I thought: the Margolises! I could get off, walk to their house, and call for a taxi from there to take me home.

"Excuse me." I got up and pushed my way past his knees. My own were trembling so hard that I could barely stand up without falling. I grabbed the back of the seat in front of us to support myself. "I'm getting off here to see some friends."

He didn't say anything, but I could feel his stare on my back as I clung to a silver pole while I waited for the train to stop and the doors to slide open. As soon as they did, I bolted off, trying not very successfully to appear less frightened than I felt. I maintained a deliberate, easy pace on my shaking knees as I walked the length of the tunnel, climbed the stairs, and emerged into the commercial heart of Brooklyn Heights.

It looked even darker and emptier than Flatbush Avenue.

I started walking in the direction I hoped was toward the promenade, guided only by the sight of the towers of the Brooklyn Bridge in the distance to my right. That, I hoped, was north, and so I needed to head slightly south and west. With every step, I looked for a cop, for a pay phone, for a taxi. No cops, no calls, no cabs. I began to walk faster and then to run, and it was then that I heard the heavy footsteps coming up fast behind me.

He reached for my shoulder as I opened my mouth to scream.

"Got you a cab," Allen Cheskey said.

I turned, winded, terrified.

Sure enough, there was a taxi at curbside.

"You looked lost," Cheskey said. "Like you needed help."

BUT I WOULDN'T WANT TO *DIE* THERE

Shit, yes, I need help! I thought, as I looked once again into his dark cold eyes. I thought of the Oriental woman's description of the murderer, or at least how her son had said that Carol's killer wore a jogging suit with a hood, which was just what a man would wear if he didn't want anybody to see that he was bald. And I thought of the owner of the Cafe O'Lay, who said his dishwasher didn't come in that day, and how Allen Cheskey had a job washing dishes at some cafe. But he ushered me into the taxi, locked the door for me, rolled down the window a bit, and gently shut the door for me.

"Take care," he called from the curb.

"Where to?" asked the cabbie.

"Riverside Drive," I said.

He glanced in his rearview mirror. "You're a long way from home."

"You can say that again."

I let myself into the apartment, expecting to find a worried, possibly angry husband waiting for me. But I didn't even find the lights turned on, just a six-pack of chocolate cupcakes with white icing waiting for me on the coffee table.

"Geof?"

No answer.

What did I expect, I asked myself, that he was taking a bath in the dark?

"Where are you?"

Had he come, got fed up already, and gone? Was his flight delayed? Had he decided to drive instead, which meant he probably wouldn't arrive until tomorrow? Was there a late-breaking case at home, so he had to stay and couldn't come to spend the weekend with me at all?

"I need you!"

I spoke to the empty air as I walked into Carol's office.

The message light was flashing, and the machine told me I had six messages. Impatiently, I played through them, hoping for one from my husband.

"This is Barbara Moore," said a resonant female voice. "I got your number from Pat Vinitsky. She said I should put undue pressure on you, so that's what I'm doing. Please. Give your approval to Andrei. Make the funding available for Book'Em. You should see me. I'm down on my knees. Raise me up, raise my kids up. Do it!"

Click.

"Where's our check? You were supposed to drop it by yesterday, you were supposed to drop it by today. Opening night is tomorrow night, for God's sake! Where's our money? This is Damon Calendar."

Click.

"This is Spidell. Remember me from the garden? This morning? The Growth Fund? Listen, I hope it's okay that I got your number from Patty Vinitsky and that I'm calling you. I just want you to know that everything went really well after you left. We bought the stuff we needed, we did so much work you wouldn't believe it, and we're just really grateful. That's all. That's all I wanted especially to say. Thanks. Thanks a lot."

Click.

"Jenny? Well, I knocked on the front door and rang the doorbell, and nobody ever came to let me in. So I got a room at the Barbizon, you know where it is on Central Park South? Why don't you just get in a cab and come on over. I've left a key at the desk for you. I miss you. I love you. See you soon, I hope."

Happiness spread over me like a blanket as I hurried to call him to let him know I was coming. Then I raced through the apartment gathering a few clothes and sundries to take with me to Geof's hotel. He was here. He didn't sound worried, he didn't sound angry. He even sounded as if he might be enjoying himself. Hot damn, I needed this. He needed this. We needed each other.

I had my hand on the knob of the inside front door when I looked back over my shoulder. The door to my landlady's apartment was open, there was light streaming out, and I heard the sound of the television. It wouldn't hurt, I thought, to take a minute to complain that Jed hadn't let my husband in as he'd promised he would. If he couldn't do it, he or his mother should have arranged to have somebody else take care of it!

I marched back down the hall and took one step into her domain.

"Hello?" I called.

Only the television replied to my inquiry.

Tentatively, I took another couple of steps down the front hallway of her apartment and paused just outside the open door of a bedroom, unsure what to do next. But damn, I was pissed, Jed had seriously inconvenienced my husband, and this time I wasn't going to delay complaining to somebody about it!

My peripheral vision caught a glimpse of something.

I turned to look into the bedroom, where all sorts of clothing was draped over every piece of furniture, falling out of the closets, dropped sloppily on the floors. There were old silk robes and old-fashioned dresses, there were shoes of all varieties and, it appeared, sizes, there were boas from another era and styles from other generations.

And my Victorian underwear.

Plain as you please, right there on the bed.

I ran in, grabbed it indignantly, and rushed back out to charge into Mrs. Goodman's living room and confront her with the evidence. But there wasn't anybody there or, apparently, anywhere else in the apartment. Rather anticlimactically, I stuck my lingerie under my arm and left the building.

Soon I was in a taxi on my way to Central Park.

24

IN THE MORNING, SWEET MORNING, WITH COOL SPRINGTIME air flowing gently through the open hotel window, I rolled my naked body over into the arms of my warm, naked husband and murmured, "Bliss." He tenderly pulled me closer, and I soaked up the heat from the furnace of his big body like a Scandinavian soaking up the sun in Spain. It was heaven. It was a sauna and a hot tub and steaming Turkish towel all wrapped around me at once, only better looking. I opened my eyes, avoided breathing into his face, and puckered my mouth onto his bristly cheek. His hands began stroking, moving, and locating familiar parts, and we began the lovely process of getting to know each other all over again.

"Still love this city?"
I buttered one of the English muffins we had ordered up from room service, and I chewed it while I pretended to consider his question. Starting with last night, I had given him a complete rundown on everything I'd done, every suspicion I'd tracked, every murderer with whom I'd ridden on a subway and every piece of clothing that anybody had tried to steal from me. I sighed dramatically, and then hoped I hadn't overplayed it.

"Okay, Geof, you win."

"I win what?"

"Me. The argument. I'll turn down the job if they offer it."

"You will?" Relief and happiness flooded his sweet, unsuspecting face, and I felt almost guilty about what I had planned for him. Machiavelli had nothing on me. "Jenny, really? You won't move here? I don't have to consider moving here? I don't even have to think about commuting here to see you on weekends? Hot damn! I knew I married a sensible woman!"

I batted my eyelashes at him demurely and thought about saying, "Yes, darling," but figured that would be one step too far in my charade of capitulation. *That* he'd never buy, and if there was one thing I didn't want this weekend, it was a suspicious, unhappy husband.

My gleeful, unsuspecting one got up from his chair, walked around the table, and gave me a bear hug.

Okay, listen, I argued with my own conscience and my better feminist nature, *I know this is manipulative as hell, but you have to understand that I spent years catering to a boardful of impossibly opinionated old men, cajoling them into thinking it was their idea to do what I wanted them to do for the foundation. Old habits die hard, especially the ones that work. So I'll reform in my next life, so give me a break, I've had a hard week.*

"Well, hell," my husband exclaimed as he padded on his bare feet back to his chair, where he began to pour coffee for me, "now I can relax and maybe even have fun this weekend, even if this is the city I will not name. What have you got lined up for us, sweetie pie?"

"It's a secret," I told him. "You'll have to wait and see."

To assuage my guilt, I left him at leisure while I got dressed and ran down to the lobby to buy a morning paper. When I got upstairs and unfolded it for us to see, we found ourselves looking at a headline that announced the death of a prominent black philanthropist early the previous evening.

"Oh, my God," I breathed, grabbing the paper to see it better.

I read with a growing sense of sadness and horror.

Dr. Malcolm Lloyd, the story said, retired surgeon, benefactor of the Growth Fund garden, and brother of the founder of the controversial Black Company, had been stabbed to death by his wife, Dorothy Lloyd, late yesterday afternoon in their condominium right down the street from our hotel.

She had used one of their African artifacts, a lance. And she was claiming self-defense.

"Could he have killed Carol?" Geof asked me.

"That's what I wondered, and so did his wife."

In fact, the story even went so far as to imply a link by describing Dr. Lloyd's battle with the Hart Foundation, his destruction of the garden, and the suggestive death of the foundation's director, Carol Margolis.

"It's out of your hands now," Geof said.

"I guess it always was." So why didn't I feel any relief, any satisfaction? "Do you mind if we wait a little while before we go out, Geof?"

"We're in no hurry, honey."

He understood: I hardly knew the Lloyds at all, but still, this latest news was a shock and confusing and I needed time to regain my equilibrium. And so we lounged around our hotel room that morning. Geof eventually found interesting ways to gently distract my mind from other people's tragedies.

We went out to a gorgeous New York Saturday.

After several days of being accused at every turn of behaving like a tourist, I finally got a chance to do what normal tourists do. I had a really good time. Geof had a *great* time because I made sure we "happened" only into galleries where I thought he'd love the current displays—like the Hieronymous Bosch show at the Metropolitan Museum of Art—that we "wandered" into stores I suspected he couldn't resist—like the little Russian jewel of a shop on Fifth Avenue where the merchandise included things like Faberge eggs, a czarina's jewelry, and a czar's cigar boxes and money clips—that we ate and drank only at the most charming cafes, and that we walked and walked and walked to remind him that regular exercise just comes naturally to a New Yorker. We held hands. We indulged in PDAs (public displays of affection) repeatedly. He even bought a disposable camera and took pictures of me against famous landmarks such as Rockefeller Center.

"You look just like a tourist," I chided him, "have you no shame?"

I wore him out—and wore down his resistance—so that by late afternoon we were forced to return to our hotel and to bed. When we finally got up, I donned my best set of new lingerie and my jingling ankle bracelet, which nearly caused us to be late to the theater.

Geof looked down at the play program, which was merely a cheaply printed single sheet of green paper. "*King Leer?*" he whispered and laughed. "I thought Shakespeare was the last bastion of literacy."

"No," I whispered back, "that's Andrei Bolen."

I felt a little guilty when I saw their badly edited program. Clearly, they needed the money, regardless of how strangely their manager/director had behaved. But how was I supposed to have gotten it to them? Slipped it under their locked doors?

The house lights were doused, plunging us all into total darkness as suddenly as if the power had gone out. Maybe it had, I thought unhappily, because maybe they hadn't been able to pay their electric bills. A riff of recorded music boomed out at us, startling us, and there were a few snickers from the packed house. This was evidently a thespian troupe that liked to shock its audiences.

"Shh," the rest of us shushed our mates.

Then the first lines of the famous play came trumpeting out at us, but the actors spoke them in still total darkness.

"*I thought the king had more affected the duke of Albany than Cornwall.*"

"*It did always appear so to us; but now, in the division of the kingdom, it appears not which of the dukes he values most; for equalities are so weighed, that curiosity in neither can make choice of either's moiety.*"

"Oh, God." Geof moaned and slumped in his seat.

Indeed, it was dreadful already, with the actors placing strange emphasis on the wrong words, like *curiosity*. At that point, the stage lights began slowly to come up, teasing us, as if somebody was barely nudging a rheostat.

We could now just barely see three figures on the stage.

"Is this not your son, my lord?"

"His breeding, sir, hath been at my charge: I have so often blushed—"

The stage lights came up fully.

My mouth dropped open fully.

A woman up front screamed.

"Oh, my *God!*" exclaimed a man on the other side of me.

The murmur from the audience grew instantly into an ocean swell that nearly drowned out the actors' next words. The actors must have been expecting that, however, because they raised their volume to compensate, much the way a comedian pauses for laughs. They got some of those, too.

"—to acknowledge him, that now I am brazed to't."

All three actors—we could now definitely see they were men—stood before us stark staring naked.

We were the ones who were staring.

Geof started laughing silently, and soon his shoulders were shaking and then his entire body was convulsed in mirth, with tears running down his face. I hadn't seen him laugh this hard since I took him to an avant-garde art show back home. A man in front of us was whooping with evident glee, and a woman in back of us kept emitting hysterical little yelps.

Meanwhile, up on the stage, Kent, Gloucester, and Edmund were joined by Lear, Cornwall, Albany, Goneril, Regan, Cordelia, and, as the script might say, attendants. All of them naked as Minerva rising from the sea. Naked, that is, except for their crowns; the royals wore crowns and carried scepters, that's how you could tell they were kings and queens. There certainly wasn't any other obvious sign; in the buff, you couldn't tell the aristocrats from the commoners.

"King Leer," I said in dumb amazement.

So this was why Carol had withheld the money!

She must have seen a dress rehearsal.

And Carol would have known immediately what conservative trustees would have to say to a lewd Lear. "No," they'd say, fifteen ways to Billy Sunday. Maybe she'd tried to get Damon Calendar to clothe his actors, and he had refused to do it. And then she'd been killed before she ever ratted on him to her trustees.

The audience—the ones who hadn't walked out already—got hysterical when Lear voiced those soon-to-be even more immortal lines: *"Which of you shall we say doth love us most? That we our largest bounty may extend—"*

My husband wiped the tears from his eyes.

"Oh, God," he said, "I love this town."

One act was enough for us.

Maybe audiences on succeeding nights (assuming there were any) would be more sophisticated than ours was; ours continued to hoop and holler like hillbillies at a hog-calling contest, while the actors seemed to really get into it, hamming it up even harder, giving the funniest possible readings to their lines.

"Want a night cap?" I asked. "There's a place on Tenth Avenue—"

Geof draped one arm around my shoulders and raised his other arm to flag down a taxi. "Lead on, MacDuff."

Steve Wolff's Saturday night gig turned out to be at a bar/restaurant. Lucille's was a small place, no bigger than fifteen tables and a long bar, with a tiny circle of space reserved in the rear for his three-piece band: Steve on keyboard and a couple of women on strings. They were playing when we walked in, but Steve noticed me and lifted his right hand from the chord he was playing to wave at me.

We took the next available table and ordered a late-night supper, starting with an appetizer of portabello mushrooms, mainly because we'd never heard of them before. When it arrived, we discovered to our delight that it was a fungi as wide and thick as a steak and grilled in garlic so it even tasted like beef.

"These could turn me into a vegetarian," Geof said.

Our next course was toasted baguettes spread with a puree of garlic, sun-dried tomatoes, basil, and goat cheese.

"I renounce meat," Geof declared.

And then our entrée arrived: spinach angel hair pasta tossed in garlic oil and pine nuts, sprinkled with Parmesan cheese, and garnished with bits of buttery soft grilled salmon.

"Jenny, why don't you get a job and move here?" Geof said.

The viola thrummed, the violin soared, and Steve's hands came down in thrilling arpeggios that somehow managed to combine haunting elements of black blues, Portuguese Fado, and new age percussion. Before the break, he spoke softly into the microphone that was attached to his music stand.

"I call this next piece 'Carol.' "

Geof reached for my hand and held on tight.

Watching Steve's head bob in time to his original music, I thought, *He's good.* As if he'd heard me, Carol's widower turned his face toward us for a moment and smiled. It, too, was spooky and memorable, like his music, a smile I'd never forget, the smile of a haunted man who had managed to turn some of his ghosts into music. Before the set was finished, I was quietly crying into the pasta left on my plate. When Geof saw that I couldn't eat any more of it, he sensitively patted my shoulder and then stole my plate, set it on top of his own empty one, and polished off the rest of my dinner for me.

Steve sat down with us afterward.

"She tell you what I need?" he asked Geof.

"I can't help you. I have no influence here. I'm sorry."

"Shit, what am I supposed to do now?"

I said, "Have you heard anything else from her parents?"

"Oh, yeah." He leaned forward, so nobody at another table could overhear us. "My lawyer has heard from them, and let me tell you, it is getting very nasty. What the *hell* am I supposed to do to convince them?" His laughter had a desperate edge to it. "I've tried telling them I'm really just a nice Jewish boy, that I call my mother once a week, and I play music for free for Jewish geriatric homes at least once a month. I'm a good boy, but they're not buying it."

"That's true?" I asked him.

"That I didn't do it?" He stared at me. "Of course, it's true!"

"No, I mean about you playing for free at retirement homes?"

"Sure, I guess a little of Carol rubbed off on me."

I was surprised to learn he ever did good works, but rather than actually say that, I remembered to tell Steve about poor Mrs. Amory in 2C, and how'd she jumped or fallen from her window and been carried off in an ambulance. Then, I complained about the curmudgeon in 5C, and while I was rolling, I started whining about the excess of baked goods coming out of 5B . . .

"Sure," Steve said, "they're all nuts."

I sighed. "And all in one place."

He looked surprised and laughed a little. "Well, of course, what did you expect from a nuthouse?"

I wasn't sure I caught his drift. "What?"

"Jenny," he said with exaggerated patience, "you don't think Carol would choose to live in a normal building with normal people if she could choose to live where she might be able to help some of life's rejects, do you? It's a nuthouse, as I think I *told* you the first day. I mean that literally, figuratively speaking. A nuthouse. Where rich mental patients go to live when they're just sane enough to be on their own and they don't have any family left who can handle them, but they have trust funds, and they're not quite crazy enough to be institutionalized." He added in a sarcastic tone, "They pay Jed's mother to keep an eye on them, and she pays him to try to keep them from plunging out of windows. Jed's the Holden Caulfield of Riverside Drive, Jenny, didn't you realize that? He tries to catch 'em just before they go over the edge. That used to make Carol furious, she thought that was a hell of a thing to ask of a teenager. Personally, I thought it was probably good for him."

I glanced at Geof; he was shaking his head, and I could just hear the thought forming in it: *This city!*

"I agree with Carol," I said to Steve. "It *is* awful."

"Oh, come on, Jenny." He laughed as he got up from our table to go play another set with his band. "Even rich crazy people need someplace to live, you know!"

After he left, I excused myself to go to the ladies' room.

Geof drained a last beer, and then we left Lucille's about fifteen minutes later, after a second rendition of "Carol." It got a nice round of applause. On the sidewalk again, Geof asked me, "Do you really think he's good enough to make it?"

Steve's music had sounded wonderful to me, but I knew there were thousands of aspiring musicians out there, and even with an album, he still had a long way to go.

"I don't have any idea," I admitted.

"He's not exactly the soul of sensitivity, is he?"

"No, but the song he wrote about Carol was nice, and he plays for old folks for free, so he can't be all bad." Something told me I ought to think a bit about that last fact, but the wine and Geof separated me from the next car on the train of my thoughts.

"We'll never catch a taxi at this hour," he predicted . . . just as one coasted to an elegantly smooth stop in front of us. We slid into the back seat of the immaculate yellow cab.

"And where," asked the spiffily dressed cabbie, "may I deliver such a handsome young couple as yourselves on this perfect evening in the Big Apple, if I may be so bold as to inquire?"

I stared at the back of his head and stifled a laugh.

Geof put his arm around me again and said in deep, regal tones, "The Barbizon Hotel on Central Park South, my good man."

"Very good, sir."

He didn't speak another word the entire trip. He drove smoothly and sanely all of the way. No honking, no cussing, no jerking into other lanes. We necked the whole route. The driver never so much as peeked in his rearview mirror. We glided to a stop in front of our hotel.

"Here we are, sir, madam."

Geof pulled out his wallet and included a generous tip with the fare.

"That's very kind of you, sir. It has been a pleasure to serve you. I wish you and the pretty lady a most pleasant remainder of the evening. Thank you so much."

I was rigidly holding onto my straight face as Geof guided me by an elbow into the lobby, where a uniformed doorman snapped to attention.

On our way up in the elevator, Geof said, "What's the rap on New York cab drivers anyway? He couldn't have been nicer if you'd paid him."

I stared straight ahead at the elevator buttons.

BUT I WOULDN'T WANT TO *DIE* THERE

The business card that the same cabbie had handed me after he drove me the other day was still nestled in my purse.

Geof and I cuddled together on a sofa pulled up to the hotel window that overlooked the lights of Central Park.

"I could get used to this," he admitted.

25

G EOF TOOK A LATE AFTERNOON FLIGHT BACK TO PORT
Frederick, following a day of sleeping late, a leisurely brunch,
and the Central Park Zoo. When I saw him off in front of the
hotel, he embraced me and said, "Maybe. If you love this job
and you really want to move here, maybe I could stand it, at
least for two or three years. It might be fun, might be good for
us. A little adventure." He laughed. "Just what you and I need,
a little more adventure in our lives. And then maybe it would
be my turn to choose—"

"Yes!" I hugged him back, so glad to have him as my ally.

"I love you!" he yelled through the open window of his cab.

Even the blasé hotel doorman looked over at me and grinned.
He could tell I was the one the good-looking man was yelling
at—I was the woman with the idiotic grin on her face.

So happy and full of confidence was I that I even took the
subway back to the Upper West Side. When I emerged, the
streetlights were just coming on. Feeling like a regular, even
a cocky, New Yorker, I turned the corner onto Riverside Drive
and walked smack into a gang of black teenage boys wearing
gang colors.

170

"Hey, it's her," one of them said, talking low.

There were six of them, much taller, much bigger than me. I recognized the speaker as the boy who'd escorted me up to Barbara Moore's office, the kid who was a fan of Machiavelli. They quickly surrounded me.

"We hear you're not going to give the money to Bolen."

"I don't know," I started to say. "I—"

"We don't think you ought to do that."

"We think you better give the dude the money."

"You listening, lady?"

I could barely hear them over the pounding in my ears. I tried to step back, but they closed in tighter. I opened my mouth to yell just as the biggest one of them reached into the inside pocket of his gang jacket, and I froze. My God, if he was going for a gun or a knife, I could be dead before anybody could help me!

Just like Carol . . .

He pulled out a paperback book.

"Once upon a time there was a Martian named Valentine Michael Smith," he read aloud. I recognized the cover; that was the opening sentence of Robert Heinlein's science fiction classic, *Stranger in a Strange Land.* The boy read a couple of paragraphs, haltingly, but he read them clear through, and then he stopped and glared down at me.

The kid next to him pulled out a book of his own and commenced to read from James Baldwin's *Native Son.*

All around the circle they went, ending with an excerpt from *The Prince,* read by my pal who thought Machiavelli would have made a great drug dealer.

The young men read with varying degrees of skill, but they all stared menacingly at me when they closed their books.

"Get it?" one of them asked me.

"Got it," I assured him.

"See ya," they muttered as they broke out of their circle.

"Pay the dude."

"He's cool."

"Nah, he ain't," said my pal as they strolled away, "but he's *cool.*"

"You, too," I murmured to the backs of their jackets.

But my hands were still shaking as I let myself into the building, and I vowed that if I ever saw their high school principal again I would kill her if this was Barbara Moore's idea of putting pressure on me. I also thought, as I so often did in this crazy city: *I have to sit down!*

The apartment building was beautifully, cheerfully lighted when I stumbled into it. Sufficiently well lighted to allow me to catch a glimpse of Jed's mother down the hall. At least, I thought that's who it was, although judging by the way this woman was attired, it might have been Scarlett O'Hara, green velvet gown and all.

"Mrs. Goodman?" I called out.

She came back to her doorway and peered at me.

"Mrs. Goodman," I said, marching toward her like Sherman to the sea, "I found my missing clothing . . . in your bedroom. Got anything to say about that?"

"Somebody found it in the trash," she said, not missing a beat, cool as Scarlett ever was. "They gave it to me. I was going to ask if it was yours."

She stood there in her ersatz Civil War finery, staring me down, obviously daring me to call her a liar.

"Who was that?"

"Who was what?"

"Who exactly found it in the trash?"

"I don't exactly remember. What were you doing in my bedroom?"

"Retrieving my lingerie," I shot back, daring her to press her luck.

She backed down, as Scarlett never would have. "Well, I'm glad you found it. Now if you don't mind, my favorite old movie is about to come on. I just love *Gone With the Wind*, don't you?"

"Mrs. Goodman, what did Jed do that even a mother can't forgive?"

She looked startled, disturbed, and then she burst out laughing.

"The little snot interrupted me in the middle of *The African Queen*," she said. "I won't stand for that, and he knows it."

BUT I WOULDN'T WANT TO *DIE* THERE

My landlady closed her door in my face.
Was there no real satisfaction to be had in this town?

The five flights of stairs up had never seemed longer, higher, and harder to climb. My encounter with the six teenagers had taken the wind clean out of me. I climbed very slowly, following an increasingly strong smell of fresh paint.

I traced it to apartment 2C, where the door was open.

"Hi," Jed called from where he stood on the rung of a ladder inside the unit. "How you doin'?"

"Okay. Are you fixing it up for Mrs. Amory? That's nice."

He stared at me. "Well, no, I mean . . . shit . . . she died, you know?"

"Oh, no! I didn't know . . ."

"So I've got to paint it and get it ready for my mom to rent out for bed and breakfast until she finds a new client."

"Jed, I'm so sorry."

"Yeah, me, too." He turned his face away and started steadily applying white paint to the wall. "I fucked up."

"It wasn't your fault!"

"Better luck next time," he said.

That left me speechless, it was such a horrifyingly cynical piece of optimism to come out of the mouth of a nineteen-year-old. With nothing more to say to him, I continued my climb to Carol's place. When I reached the door, I unlocked it and opened it cautiously, having grown wary in my time in New York.

"Well, hello," I said and nearly laughed.

Because, sure enough, there was a man in my room.

"Mr. Bread," I said to my elderly neighbor from 5C. "What are you doing here?"

26

HE LOOKED LIKE A CRANKY OLD RABBIT, CORNERED BY headlights. This rabbit wore house slippers, baggy wool trousers, and a sweatshirt, but the most eccentric element of his attire was the large, stained, once-white apron he had tied about his neck and waist, not to mention the extremely tall and puffy chef's hat that sat atop his balding head.

In his hands, he held the evidence.

"Are those cookies for me, Mr. Bread?"

He lowered his head, his eyes darting frantically, the rabbit looking for escape from the merciless, snarling dog. And I was just about snarling by that time; I was not charmed by this game he'd been playing with me, he and Mrs. Golding.

"You're the fifth-floor baker, aren't you?"

He began edging around the furniture, but I didn't budge out of his way, so he couldn't edge his way out of the room yet.

"You left the basket of goodies in the refrigerator, didn't you? And all those cakes and muffins and little loaves of bread?"

I was the rigid fence that stood between him and freedom.

"Why don't you want anybody to know it?"

"He's shy," said a trembling voice behind me.

I turned, and there was his co-conspirator. She looked truly

174

frightened. Suddenly, seeing her response to my anger, my cold heart melted, for how could I stay angry at them?

"Oh, hell," I said, giving up and smiling at her, "come on in, Mrs. Golding, I'll pour us all some milk and we'll eat the damn cookies!"

"He was a baker," Mrs. Golding told me, as he still wasn't talking much, except to snap at her whenever she tried to embroider around the truth of their tale. We were sitting at Carol's little table, with crumbs all around us. "You probably think he changed his name, because of his profession, but he didn't. He was born Daley, and that's how he knew what his profession should be. A man named Daley Bread, he has to become a baker, that was always obvious to him, even from the time he was a little child."

I could see that she was impressed by that.

"He always worked in bakeries, he was good, but then they retired him, and he didn't have any work to do anymore. So wherever he lived after that, he made things for people. But before he met me, he never gave the people the things he made for them."

I held up my hand. "He baked things but kept them?"

"Yes." Even he nodded at that; this, he confirmed, was accurate.

"But then he moved here," she said, "and I saw what the problem was, so I said I'd be his delivery boy."

For the first time, he spoke. "Takes the credit."

"I *have* to," she screeched at him. "Or they'd all *know!*"

"What about the hall lights?" I asked him. "Is that you, too?"

His glance darted toward her. "Dirty liar."

"I can't *tell!*" she cried. "If I *tell*, it'll happen to *me!*"

"What will happen to you, Mrs. Golding?"

"Die," she said.

"What?" I stared at her.

"I'll die," she said clearly, only softer this time.

The chill that suddenly went through me traveled clear to my bones.

And then, click, click, click, certain pieces of information rolled like little metal balls down the slot of a pinball machine that heaved and rattled and then screamed "TILT" in my brain.

It took me a moment to regain my ability to breathe.

I could still smell the fresh paint from downstairs. I took a very deep breath before I said: "Mrs. Golding, what happened to the person who lived in this apartment before Carol and Steve stayed here on their honeymoon?"

"Died," she whispered.

Our neighbor shifted uneasily in his chair.

"How did he—she?—die, Mrs. Golding?"

"She." It was the barest whisper. "Don't remember."

"And just before Carol Margolis was killed . . . was there a death, here in this building, another one of the tenants?"

"Drowned," she said. "In the tub."

There was Carol's "problem": A mentally ill tenant had died—in this illegal boarding house—which *appeared* to do a lot of good.

"How long have you lived here, Mrs. Golding?"

But she didn't seem to remember the answer to that and merely shook her head in a frantic way.

"How many residents have died since you've been here?"

"Some," she said.

"They was old!" he yelled suddenly, so that she and I jumped back in our chairs. "We're old! They died, just like we'll die if I don't kill you first! Dying's natural, like sugar and vanilla, and you're just a crazy old lady!"

"Not!" she screamed back. "Am not!"

She started making such a commotion and I was so busy frantically trying to hush her that neither she nor I heard the keys turn in my locks. It was only because of the look on Daley Bread's face that we two women became aware that another man had entered the room.

Mrs. Golding gasped and clutched my hands.

"Ida," Jed Goodman said, "and Daley, why don't you go back to your rooms now?"

I hadn't even gotten the chance to ask her my next question, which was going to have been: What's Jed's other part-time job? Is it washing dishes at the Cafe O'Lay, where the dishwasher didn't get to work on time the night that Carol was killed?

"Will you leave the hall lights on for us?" she asked, her lips trembling like a frightened child's.

"Maybe. But only if you both hurry and go right now."

With guilty, frightened glances for me, they both got up quickly from their chairs and scooted past me, then past their young doorman. Without any backward glances, they raced out of Carol's apartment, and Jed quietly closed the door behind them and locked it.

"Stop," he commanded, for I had got up from my own chair and started to move quietly toward the sofa, where I knew that a small caliber pistol rested in a drawer, though its ammunition was scattered uselessly about. "Right there."

I was halfway between the table and the long window.

He and I looked at each other, sizing things up.

"Why Carol?"

"She was going to report us for running an unlicensed place. That meant an investigation."

"How many others?" I asked him.

"It doesn't matter," he said.

"When was the first?"

"When I was nine. It was kind of an accident. One of Mom's crazy old tenants was in the tub and she started having a heart attack, I guess, and I followed Mom in to help her. And when Mom went to call for some help, the old lady started thrashing around in the tub and I just kind of grabbed her feet to try to keep her from hurting herself"—he laughed a little—"only it pulled her head under the water, and I found out that people drown really fast like that. You'd be surprised. But that wasn't the biggest surprise. The real shock was how much I enjoyed it." He stared at me. "It was, like, fun. It was, like, really thrilling, you know?"

"Your mother, she knows?"

He shrugged. "She likes the clothes."

I thought that was the single most cold-blooded thing I'd ever heard anybody say. And, it occurred to me, maybe ever would hear. Like Daley before me, I started edging around the room again. But Jed came at me on the run, and I started screaming, which lasted only the few seconds before he grabbed me and slapped his big hand over my mouth and pinioned my arms to my body. While I desperately tried to bite him, to twist away from him, to kick him, he dragged me toward the open window.

Through my own eyelashes, I saw the death membrane glistening.

In a moment, the fronts of my legs were touching the windowsill. Then he had me bent over, hanging halfway out. Five stories below, his mother was sitting in semidarkness on her patio.

Soon, I'd be joining her there.

"Jenny!"

At the sound of another voice, Jed's grasp loosened for a moment but not long enough for me to get away. He still had a fierce grip on me when he and I whirled enough to see Steve Wolff standing in the doorway, his doorkeys still dangling from his fingers.

"My God, Jenny! Don't jump! Stop her, Jed!"

Behind him came the cavalry with the heavy artillery: It was Ida Golding and Daley Bread, armed with dozens of cookies and muffins, which they hurled like grenades at the combatants at the window.

At that point—when his mother down below finally heard us above and craned her head toward us—Jed just gave up. He surrendered to the inevitable, I think. He dropped my arms, stepped back away from me, and began to laugh hysterically. Unfortunately, he released me so abruptly that I nearly plunged on through the window anyway, and it was only Steve, diving for the floor and grabbing my foot, who saved me.

Later, I asked him, "What were you doing here?"

"I came over to ask you to dinner," he said in an aggrieved, whining kind of voice. "I thought it was my turn. But, geez."

Epilogue

I STAYED ON IN CAROL'S PLACE FOR THE REMAINDER OF THAT week and the next, finishing my interim job. On my last Friday, Patty Vinitsky took me to lunch and told me that her board had voted to offer me the job on a permanent basis.

"It's yours," she said.

"Well, God," I retorted, "I should hope so!"

She laughed very hard at that and then pressed her offer.

"Patty," I asked, "why do you like Book'Em so much?"

"What do you mean, why?"

"Is it Andrei? He's cute, I'll grant you, but—"

"Oh, please." She looked disgusted with me. "Has it occurred to you that I might actually believe in the need for literacy among our high school students, that I might even believe in it passionately?"

No, I thought humbly, *Actually, it hadn't.*

"So why'd you leave your old job?" she asked me.

"I don't have to tell you."

"What?"

"I'm not applying for the position."
She stared at me. "You don't want it?"

I didn't want it.

I'd learned that I didn't want to work for anybody else; I wanted to work for myself. And I figured the best way to do that was to start a foundation of my own with family money and other friendly contributions, and I wanted to do that back home to benefit my hometown. From Port Frederick, I could travel anywhere I wanted to go for all the excitement in the world. But I could also keep my cottage, and my dear husband could keep doing the work he loved exactly where he wanted to keep doing it. That's where we'd both be happy, and it was no sacrifice to admit it; on the contrary, it was a pleasure to be so sure.

And so, on the beautiful Sunday morning following that Friday lunch with Pat, I got a taxi to take me to City Hall Park. I was flying home that evening, but Marty and Esther Margolis had invited me to have lunch with them in their home in Brooklyn Heights.

As I got out of the cab, I looked up and saw the suspension wires of the Brooklyn Bridge shining beautifully in the morning sunlight. It was cool out, so I'd worn my trench coat and brought along a head scarf in case the wind picked up on the bridge.

Steve Wolff was there to meet me; he was going, too.

My driver said, "Sure you don't want me to drive you across?"

"No," I told him, returning his smile. "We'll walk."